LUCK MAKER

KISMET ACADEMY

SARAH BIGLOW

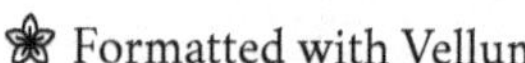 Formatted with Vellum

CHAPTER ONE

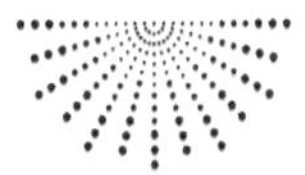

The only place I'd ever felt normal was in the back office of my family's restaurant crammed in beside my grandmother as she prepared the day's messages. By the time I was eight years old I could expertly slide them into fortune cookies. I loved those afternoons after school where I'd study her neat script as she put pen to slips of paper. She'd whispered stories all of my life about how our family had magic in our blood and it was our honor and our duty to use it to help people. I'd clung to those stories as a little girl, because it gave me hope that I would one day amount to more than being the disappointment I saw in my father's eyes every day.

I'd fleetingly hoped when I turned thirteen that something would happen. That some power would manifest, but nothing had happened. I'd managed to hide my heartbreak from everyone and thrown myself into school, hoping excelling in academics would make up for my lack of magic. By the time I hit my freshman year of college, that belief in magic had died.

Summer had finally arrived, and I was on my way back home to see my grandmother. Our weekly phone calls weren't enough. I might have outgrown my belief in the family magic, but that didn't mean I didn't treasure our time together. The scents of the city—car exhaust, smoke from the grates above the subway, and street food sizzling on carts—welcomed me home as I walked the three blocks from the nearest subway station to the restaurant. I could see the red awning with the name 'Zhou's' emblazoned in gold script fluttering in the breeze. It brought a smile to my lips and a sense of peace washed over me. *I was home.* My feet carried me along the familiar path, bypassing the front of the establishment and ducking down the side street to the back of the building and the employee entrance.

The moment my fingers touched the cool metal of the door handle, my heart skipped a beat. I couldn't explain why, but something felt *off.* Normally, the ambiance of the restaurant filtered out even when the doors were closed. But it was eerily silent as I pulled the door outward.

"Hello?" I called, stepping into the short hall that led to the kitchen and the back office.

No response.

My stomach did a somersault as I realized none of the staff were there. I had been gone for months, but surely, they hadn't changed the hours on me. There should have been a half dozen chefs and prep cooks flitting around the industrial-sized kitchen. Yet every stove top and oven sat cold and unused. I could see half-prepared food sitting on the counters. People had been here not long ago. There was no way in hell my father would let the staff leave their stations in such disarray. *What's going on?*

"*Nai-Nai*, are you here?" My voice cracked on the last word, icy tendrils of unease crept down my back and coiled in my belly.

Above me, the lights blinked out and back on again, and it stopped me in my tracks. "Get a hold of yourself, Mae Lin," I chided. Power flickered all the time. Still, the abandoned kitchen had to mean something.

Forcing myself onward, I stepped into the back office. I could see my grandmother's organizational skills at play. She had neat little rows of fortunes ready to be slipped inside cookies for the day's patrons. Nothing in the room suggested she'd left in a hurry.

The lighting sputtered overhead again, plunging the office into temporary darkness. As I waited for the power grid to reset itself, I caught the scent of something sharp and cloying, like the air after an electrical storm. The dining room was the only place left to check.

Part of me didn't want to leave the safety of the office. Though if something was going on, I owed it to my family to do what I could to protect the restaurant. Swallowing the lump in my throat I reached out a hand, groping in the darkness until I made contact with the wall. Once I was in the space between the office and the kitchen, I pressed my body against the wall, inching forward step by step until I reached the deep mauve curtain separating the dining room from the kitchen.

"I told you not to come here," Nai-Nai's voice was sharp. In my nineteen years of life, I'd never heard her raise her voice with anyone.

"And you know I will do as I please," a deep male voice responded.

"You have no reason to be here. We have nothing to discuss," Nai-Nai responded. I heard fabric rustle and I peered through the curtain in spite of myself. I noticed as she gathered her skirt and turned away from whoever this strange man was.

"You think I came here to discuss anything?" The man's voice slid into a sneer on the second to last word. "I came for what I'm owed."

"I owe you *nothing*," she answered.

Floorboards groaned beneath someone's shifting weight and I heard my grandmother gasp. Breath caught in my throat, as if I, too, shared the pain I saw etched in her features. I knew she needed help, but I was powerless to intervene. My body had betrayed me and my fingers let the curtain flutter back into place. A different scent replaced the cloying ozone in my nose. Something spicy, but not anything my brain could identify in that moment. The sliver of floor visible beneath the curtain flashed bright and red. A flicker of something golden followed, only weaker.

The sound of weight hitting the floor spurred me forward and I burst through the curtain to find my grandmother laying on the floor, clutching at her chest. I could see a dribble of blood marring the corner of her mouth. A man I'd never seen before hovered over her and I could swear his entire aura glowed red. I tried to commit his image to memory.

He had dark features and a slender build. If he'd been ten years younger, he might have been attractive.

I fell to my knees beside my grandmother, reaching for her hand. "*Nai-Nai*, I'm here," I said, leaning in close so she could see and hear me.

"You were not supposed to be here," she whispered, her voice suddenly hoarse.

"Shh, just rest. I'm going to call an ambulance," I soothed. I had no idea what this man had done to her, but I knew she needed help.

I reached for my phone and dialed 9-1-1. As the line rang, I looked up, intent on telling the man to not move. Except he was gone. I hadn't heard the bell above the front door ring to announce his exit.

"Where did he go?" I blurted as the line clicked over to an emergency operator.

"9-1-1, what is your emergency?"

"I need help. My grandmother, she's been attacked. I need an ambulance."

I rattled off the address as I crouched beside my grandmother. Trying to pull her head into my lap before realizing I had no idea what had happened and I could be making any injuries worse.

"Stay on the line until paramedics arrive. They are five minutes out," the dispatcher said.

"Okay," I answered, almost on autopilot.

I set the phone down and turned my attention to the woman beside me. "Who was that man? What did he want?"

What did he do to you?

From her position on the floor, she shook her head and let out a cough. Blood dripped further down her cheek and I reached to wipe it away on instinct. "I am sorry, Mae Lin. I thought I could keep all of this away from you."

"What are you talking about?" My voice cracked at the end without meaning to.

"You are so very important. More than you know. I wish I had time to explain," she rasped, reaching her hands up to clasp mine.

"You're not making sense, *Nai-Nai*. You'll have plenty of time to tell me whatever it is. The ambulance is almost here."

"You must learn to harness what is within you. You must learn to use our family's gift. It is the only way ..." she trailed off.

It had to be a trick of light, because I could swear her entire body glowed amber. Just like the man had cast a hazy red aura before he vanished. Her hands grew warm in mine and all at once, my body thrummed with energy. It was as if someone had dosed me with a caffeine drip, supercharging my senses. The feeling faded within seconds along with the glow.

It's just adrenaline.

In the distance, sirens wailed. She just had to hold on a little longer. Then they could get her to the hospital, and she would be fine. Brakes screeched outside the front of the restaurant. I heard the slam of doors and voices calling out.

"In here," I yelled just as my grandmother's breath rattled ominously in her chest.

The front door opened, the tiny bell announcing the paramedics arrival. They rushed in, ushering me out of the way as they examined her. A man with greying temples looked at me.

"What happened?"

"I don't know. There was a man. I think he hurt her. I didn't see …" Tears burned the backs of my eyes as I watched them work.

Footsteps pounded on the pavement and my father appeared in the open doorway, his slender blue tie whipping in the wind. Even when he didn't have to, he wore a suit and tie. No one expected him to dress up just to prove he was an entrepreneur. But today, in this moment, that constant was comforting.

"What happened?" he demanded.

I couldn't answer. I just rushed over, throwing my arms around him. We stood there as the medics worked on my grandmother, hooking her up to a portable heart monitor. The high-pitched drone of a flatline buzzed like an angry insect in my ears.

She was gone.

THE FUNERAL HAD BEEN WELL-ATTENDED a week after my grandmother's death. The police had even come to take a statement about what I'd witnessed. I knew there was nothing they could do. We didn't have cameras in the restaurant that could have shown what had happened. Nearly two months had passed without any viable leads. The police weren't going to get justice for her. I had no idea how I was going to manage it, but I vowed to track down the man who'd taken her from us.

"We need to increase back to full dinner service, don't you think?" my father said, pulling me from the darkness of my thoughts. He sat in the chair behind the desk in the restaurant's back office. He'd been working late here every night for weeks, even though we were partially closed as a sign of mourning.

"Whatever you think is right, *bàbā*," I answered. It mattered little to me. I'd be going back to college in a week and he'd never cared about my opinion before now.

"Mae Lin, I know you are grieving. But now that your grandmother is gone, I need you to step up and help."

I glared at him. "You're the one who's run this business for the last twenty years. I have finished two semesters of college. And it's not like you've ever cared about my opinion before," I snapped.

On instinct, I bowed my head and averted my gaze. A daughter wasn't supposed to argue with or contradict her parents. It was dishonorable. But with the way he'd gone about things like business as usual —with the restaurant being more important than the fact his own mother was dead—infuriated me.

I expected him to yell back at me; to tell me I had no right to speak to him in such a manner. It wouldn't have been the first time he'd scolded me for being disobedient. Instead, he set his pen and notepad down then pushed the chair away from the desk. He rose to his full height and pulled me into a hug. It was such an uncommon gesture, it caught me off guard and I tensed against the embrace.

"I miss her, too, you know. I am just trying to

make her proud and do what I think she would want to keep this place alive in her memory."

My shoulders sagged. "I understand. I'm sorry. I'm just angry. The police did nothing, and I feel like it's all my fault. If I'd seen more or done something, maybe she'd still be alive."

"You cannot blame yourself or change the past. I do not know the man you saw, but from what you described, we are lucky he didn't hurt you. I am grateful that I didn't lose you, too."

I glanced around the office. There was more to running this place than I'd realized growing up. It had all looked so simple from a child's perspective. "Maybe I should skip fall semester. So, I can help out around here. I'm sure I can convince the school to defer my enrollment until spring."

"No. I will manage here. You need to go to school. Getting your degree is what she would have wanted."

Somehow, I doubted that was true. She'd wanted me to be happy, yes. Only I think she'd known I had gone into my chosen field of study out of a sense of family obligation. "We should open up for full service. Take out, delivery, all of it," I said, hoping agreeing with his plan would keep him in good spirits.

He leaned down and kissed my cheek. "Good. I need to go do inventory."

I watched him disappear toward the kitchen and sunk into the vacated chair. If I closed my eyes and sat still, I could almost feel my grandmother's presence around me. It felt … *restless.*

I'm going to find you peace, Nai-Nai.

Out of the corner of my eye, something flashed golden by my left hand. The light shimmered, settling on the handle of the drawer. I blinked, expecting the light to die down. Though it only intensified, seeming to pull my hand toward it. I eased it open and stared at the contents—some spare pens and slips of paper for the fortune cookies. If this was my grandmother trying to nudge me in a direction, I was going to need more.

"What am I looking for?" I whispered to the stillness around me.

My left hand twitched of its own accord, disturbing the pens until the corner of a slim envelope appeared. I retrieved it to find my name on it in my grandmother's neat handwriting on the front. I flipped it over and tried to slide my finger beneath the flap to open it, but it wouldn't budge. I rooted around in the drawer for a letter opener, but it was as if the envelope were made of metal itself. The tip of the opener dented.

What is going on?

Fresh tears pricked at my eyes as I stared at my name in her handwriting. I was meant to find this message, yet I couldn't open it. How did that help anything?

"I wish I knew what I'm supposed to do now."

"I think I may be able to help in that regard," an accented male voice said from the doorway.

CHAPTER TWO

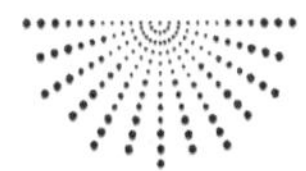

Panic tightened my chest and cemented my body to the chair. I stared at a slender red-haired man who'd just appeared in the doorway out of nowhere. My heart hammered in my throat, making it impossible to swallow or breathe as my brain tried to sort through what was going on. *How had he gotten here? How had he heard my question?* He seemed content to stand there while I sat speechless. He leaned on the doorframe as if he belonged here.

"H-how did you get in here?" I stuttered, forcing my vocal cords to work.

The man's lips quirked up into a smile before his face fell. "Oh, you're serious … you've no idea how I got here or who I am, do you?"

"Of course, I don't!" My voice pitched up on the

last word. Finally I regained control of my extremities and jumped to my feet, the chair skittering back behind me. I took half a step toward the door before realizing that I couldn't get past him. "I'm going to give you five seconds to get out of here before I call the police."

"Ms. Zhou, I didn't mean to alarm you. I was simply answering your call for help."

"I didn't ..." I trailed off. I had said I'd wished I knew what came next. But that couldn't have summoned a complete stranger. Yet, it seemed I wasn't a stranger to him. My brain tried to rationalize that information. My family name was emblazoned on the restaurant. It wasn't a huge leap for him to assume anyone in the back office was family and carried the same name.

"I was an acquaintance of your grandmother," he offered. "My name is Dr. Ronan O'Sullivan."

"She never mentioned you," I answered, expecting the conversation to draw my father's attention, yet he didn't appear. *Had this man done something to my father to gain entry?*

He gave me another sad smile. The expression tugged at the edges of his immaculately trimmed beard, threaded with veins of grey. "I'm not surprised, we knew one another a long time ago during our school days. Which is why I am here."

Part of me wanted to reach for the desk phone and call the police, but a larger part driven by curiosity wanted to hear what else this man had to say. Nai-Nai had never really talked about her youth and school. Still, it seemed this man would have stuck out in a Chinese school. "I'm listening."

"I am the Dean of Students for Kismet Academy," he paused, "which by your look of confusion I assume you have never heard of it either." He waved a hand dismissively before I could speak. "It is an educational institution aimed at honing the skills of djinn, leprechauns like myself, and wishers, like you and your grandmother."

"Those were all words I conceptually understand as English, but they made absolutely no sense," I blurted, immediately regretting the words.

"You carry a great gift in your blood, young lady, and the time has come for you to learn to use it."

"Gift?"

He sighed. "Magic, my dear. Your family's power."

"You're telling me … that magic is real?"

"Why would it be so far-fetched? Surely your grandmother told you of your family's abilities."

"When I was a kid, sure. But those were just stories. They weren't real."

"That, I'm afraid, just isn't true. Come with me, I'd like to show you what awaits you."

"What *awaits* me is my second year at college, earning the business degree my father expects me to get," I retorted.

"Just come to the campus and see what could be your future. Then, if you decide it isn't for you, you can tell me to piss off and I'll leave your family in peace," he challenged.

"How far is it?"

"Oh, not a long trip," he answered and pulled something rocklike out of his pocket. "Now, mind you keep your arms and legs inside at all times."

I gaped at him as he set the rock on the floor. This man was insane. He'd given me no real proof that my grandmother had known him or that she would have approved of me running off with him to who knows where. Yet, that odd golden glow that had drawn me to the drawer and her letter to me reappeared, practically forming a flashing arrow pointing at the rock. It seemed to sparkle with an inviting emerald hue. There was a chance this man was about to magically abduct me, but I had to believe that my grandmother's spirit was at work here. If I had magic it could help me get her justice, I owed it to both of us to see if what this man said was true.

"Okay. I'll come, but I'm not promising anything," I said, making sure her letter was still firmly tucked in my pocket.

"Understood." Dr. O'Sullivan answered and snapped his fingers.

Brilliant multicolored light filled the tiny office and a massive rainbow shot forth from the tiny rock. It undulated on its own accord until it found the window facing the street and the end disappeared beyond the glass. A snort of disbelief passed my lips, but he didn't seem to mind. Maybe he'd even expected that reaction.

"This is crazy," I repeated as he offered me his hand.

He gave my fingers a gentle squeeze and pulled me in close before taking a step into the light. The office vanished instantly and for a brief moment we tumbled through pure white light. Between one blink and the next, it resolved into a mountain range in the distance and lush greenery framing tall ornate metal gates. The center was adorned with three figures that looked human if a bit stylized.

"Welcome to Kismet Academy, Ms. Zhou," Dr. O'Sullivan stated and eased the gates open.

"Where are we?" I whispered in awe.

"Technically, not far from the Berkshires," he said with a shrug. "But we're hidden from prying eyes."

"How long has this place been here?"

"Only a few hundred years. There are academies around that are far older. One down off the coast of Georgia has been around for millennia."

"How is that even possible?"

"I suppose time works differently when you're angelic," he said with another one-shouldered shrug, as if that should explain everything.

I chose not to dwell on the fact he'd just referenced angels. There was only so much I could handle and the divine on top of somehow transporting myself through a rainbow to a magical school was miles beyond my limit.

"This way. I'll give you the penny tour," he called.

I had to do a double step to catch up with him. I tried to take in everything around me. The grounds were devoid of people, which if it kept to a similar schedule to regular universities then classes wouldn't be in session yet.

"We offer a three-year training program which prepares you to use your gifts as well as harness basic magic," O'Sullivan said, drawing my attention away from the rolling hills to the large building that loomed ahead of us. It was made of weathered stone —limestone maybe—and rose up six stories.

"You said something about the type of people that come here," I said.

"Yes, we are open to djinn, leprechauns, and wishers. All have innate magic tied to the control of luck or destiny."

Kismet makes sense now.

"And how do you know if someone is one of those?"

He let out a long breath. "I see, we will need to make sure you enroll in our Introduction to Magic course. Don't worry, you're not the only one who has come to us with a sorely lacking foundation."

My shoulders stiffened at the dig and his facial features softened when he looked back at me. "I didn't mean it as an offense."

Dr. O'Sullivan continued on toward the large building and I had no choice but to follow. As strange as this experience was, some part of me felt comfortable here. Or at least I thought I could be. It wasn't that I felt out of place at college. Though if I were being honest with myself, there was something missing from my classes. Some connection I couldn't put my finger on that wasn't there. *Is this what's been missing?*

"We hold classes from September to June each year. Students are expected to reside on campus during school terms."

"Is there anything like work study?" If I was going to convince my father that such a change to my education was going to happen, I needed to come prepared with all of the reasons he should agree to let me go. Having a way to earn money while I was away would help. Especially with the restaurant having been at half working capacity for the last two months.

"I'm afraid there's not much time for work beyond your studies while you're here." He glanced up at the ornate double doors of the building and gave me a wink. "And if it's money that concerns you, fear not. As a legacy admission, your tuition is covered already."

"Legacy? You mean my dad went here, too?"

"Not exactly." He tugged the heavy doors open and ushered me inside. Given the stone exterior, I expected to find a drafty interior, but it was comfortable. I looked for signs of air conditioning ducts or venting, but nothing obvious appeared. Dr. O'Sullivan led me to a wall of framed photographs and pointed to one hanging near the bottom of a cluster. "That was me and your grandmother in our last year here."

I bent to study the photo. It certainly looked like my grandmother. She was thinner and her hair fuller, but she had the same smile that made her eyes twinkle. She looked so proud standing there beside a red-haired young man in matching red blazers.

"As I said, your grandmother and I attended school together."

"And because I'm her family, I get in. No fees, just because?"

"That's how it works."

"Then, why didn't my dad tell me I should come here?"

"I don't want to venture into your family dynamic. But the way in which your family's magic operates, it's possible he didn't know about the school."

My temples throbbed with the influx of information. "I don't understand."

"Wisher magic is hereditary, as all luck-based magic is, except unlike djinn or leprechauns, the gift must be willingly passed from one family member to another."

The golden glow and the electrical charge that

day in the restaurant suddenly flooded my memory. My fingertips tingled at the sense memory and a pale glow wafted off my skin like steam. "But she would have meant to give it to my father."

"If she was anything like the girl I knew, she didn't do anything without purpose. If you came to possess her gift, it was because she intended you to have it."

"She always told me I was special, but I never really believed her."

"I swear to you, we will teach you everything you need to know about how to manifest your gifts and harness the magic that is your birthright, Ms. Zhou. We've had a spot open for you for some time. I do hope you will sincerely consider accepting our offer of admission." He paused, let out a prolonged sigh and added, "I think your grandmother would have been very happy if you came to join us."

"When do I have to decide?" I couldn't take my eyes off the photograph on the wall.

"Term starts September first."

That left me with two weeks to decide whether to abandon the path I'd been on or blaze a new one, to honor *Nai-Nai* and find a way to track down her killer.

'*Mae Lin ...*'

An ethereal voice whispered my name like it had been carried by some distant wind all the way here. It wasn't my *Nai-Nai's* voice though. It wasn't one I recognized, and yet it felt somehow familiar. It carried a note of pleading as if it would be horribly hurt if I chose not to attend. My head whipped toward the direction my ears assumed it had come, but it faded too quickly.

"Feel free to explore the grounds a bit. Dormitories are on the fifth and sixth floors. Same sex assignments, of course. I'll be in the Dean's office on the third floor when you're ready to go back home," Dr. O'Sullivan said.

He left me in the foyer with the picture of our shared history. The vastness of the building surrounding me was its own lure, promising untold mysteries around every corner and beyond every door. And yet, whatever had called to me wasn't in this building. I couldn't explain how I knew it, but I did.

Retracing my steps, I wandered down the lush grass to a small pond where a mother duck paddled along the surface, trailed by four little ducklings. They regarded me for a moment before dipping their beaks beneath the water looking for food.

"Please tell me if this is where I'm meant to be," I

whispered. My hand absently reached into my pocket and my fingers brushed against the envelope I'd discovered just before Dr. O'Sullivan's arrival. Here seemed as fine a place as any to see if I could try again to open the message *Nai-Nai* had left for me.

Maybe it was the slight dampness in the air from the pond, but the flap came free this time as I slid my finger along its edge. A single small slip of paper waited inside. It was the same paper she had used for the cookies at the restaurant.

Embrace your gifts, wherever they may take you.

It certainly read like one of the fortunes she'd pass out to our patrons. But the ink looked darker than normal. I flipped the paper over to find a second message, this time with my name preceding the rest of the text.

Mae Lin, be mindful of what history may seek to show you. Not all questions are meant to be answered.

There was no way I would figure out what that meant sitting in a sophomore business economics class at college. Dr. O'Sullivan was right. She would have wanted me to come here, to learn how to use her last gift.

I returned to the building and took the first set of stairs to the third floor. Thankfully, the Dean's office was well marked and easy to find. I knocked on the door and waited.

"Come in," Dr. O'Sullivan's voice rang out.

I nudged the door inward with my toe and crossed the threshold. "I'm ready to go. And I want to be here on September first … I need to be here." The confidence in my sudden decision faltered. "How exactly do I get back here on my own?"

He pointed to a black case with the emblem from the front gates emblazoned on it in gold trim. "That will have everything you need. Gates open for new student admittance promptly at nine o'clock. Don't be late."

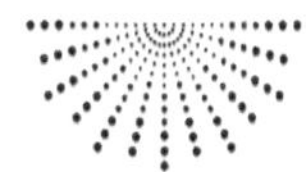

"You can't just go," my father argued as the clock ticked past eight forty on the morning of September first.

I'd studied the contents of the case repeatedly. It contained school uniforms which didn't thrill me, a formal letter of acceptance, a declaration that no tuition was in fact due, and a tiny rainbow rock to get me there, along with instructions on how to use it. I had also packed a suitcase of regular clothes just to be on the safe side.

"Yes, I can. I've already spoken with the Admissions Department at school and they've agreed to refund fall tuition. They even said they could hold my spot for the year. I think they felt guilty about *Nai-Nai* dying so they were being generous," I explained as I checked the zipper on my suitcase for the fifth time in the last ten minutes.

"This is not what we agreed on," he protested.

I straightened. "No, but things change, *bàbā*. And I know that *Nai-Nai* would want me to do this. She left me a message before she died."

"What message?" The exasperation in his tone only served to irritate me.

I retrieved the message I'd stowed in the school case and let him see it. He studied the neatly written text on both sides of the paper before handing it back to me. "I see nothing I say is going to stop you."

"I promise, I'll come back on breaks. I'm not abandoning the restaurant or you. I just need to see where this takes me. She would want me to live my life and that's what I'm going to do."

"At least let me take you," he insisted.

"I have a way there. I told you about the magic," I reminded him.

My phone alarm beeped at me, letting me know I had only ten minutes to get to my destination before I was officially late for my first term at Kismet Academy. I refused to start the year off with a bad impression. I leaned in and gave my father a kiss on the cheek before I picked up the stone from the case. According to the instructions, I just had to point it toward a window and think of my destination then the rainbow would activate. I only hoped it wouldn't entirely freak out my father. "See you for Christmas," I said as the prism effect burst forth from the rock and cast a path to the start of this new journey.

AIR FLED my lungs as I stepped onto the grounds and my stomach sloshed with the sudden displacement. I sucked in several deep breaths to quell my nausea and looked around. Other students popped up out of thin air, not all out of rainbows though. Some were accompanied by older relatives. I scanned the faces, just trying to take in the people who would become my classmates. I spotted several with Asian features while others sported pale skin and reddish-brown hair. Still others were darker skinned with an almost visible aura around them in every hue imaginable. I had a guess as to which groups they belonged to, but I didn't want to voice my assumptions.

I shouldered the case and dragged my suitcase behind me as the gates opened of their own accord—they were probably just remote controlled—and students began funneling through onto the grounds.

I couldn't help feeling out of place, even though by all accounts, I belonged here.

I reached the front of the school building in the middle of the pack and waited as Dr. O'Sullivan appeared along with other older adults, I assumed were professors. O'Sullivan beamed down at everyone, turning his head as if to meet each student's gaze in turn. It had to be my imagination that he lingered on me before turning his attention elsewhere. He was dressed as he'd been during our first meeting in a neat grey suit and tie with an emerald green vest poking out beneath his jacket lapels.

"Welcome everyone. We will be holding a brief orientation after everyone gets settled in their dorms. Please see Dr. Shen for room assignments." A short Asian woman with purple streaks in her hair held up a hand and waved a list above her head.

The other people who'd flanked O'Sullivan and Shen moved through the assembled student body, greeting people. I pushed my way to the front of the line in front of Dr. Shen.

"Name?" she said, gazing at me over the top of her list.

"Mae Lin Zhou," I answered, trying not to let the nervous energy coursing through me overcome me.

"We were wondering when you'd be joining us,"

she noted. I could hear the smile in her voice. "You're in room six eighteen." She reached into her pocket and handed me a small silver key.

I pocketed it and headed inside. I lingered just long enough to hear the person behind me get their room assignment; Lee Wu in room six forty. I struggled to get my suitcase up the first flight of stairs before I heard footsteps thundering behind me. I pressed myself to the wall to get out of the way when a handsome guy about my age appeared. He sported close-cropped dark hair and wire-rimmed glasses.

"Sorry, you can go ahead of me," I offered, noting he didn't have any luggage.

"I was actually going to ask if you wanted help," he said and pointed to my suitcase.

A blush crept over my cheeks and I gave a nervous hiccup of laughter. "Thanks."

"I'm Lee," he said as he picked up the bottom of the suitcase.

"Mae Lin," I replied, awkwardly offering him my hand to shake.

"I think we're on the same floor," he said.

Had he been listening to my room assignment?

Then again, it wasn't like I hadn't heard his assignment, too. We stopped on the fourth floor to catch our breath and I caught sight of the pond out the nearest window. The little voice that had called my name tickled the back of my mind. It was like whatever had enticed me to stay, knew I was back.

"So, how long have you known about all of this?" I waved my hand in an all-encompassing gesture.

His brow knit together over the top of his glasses. "Since forever. What, you didn't?"

I hung my head. "No."

"So, you just got your power and didn't know it was coming? No warning?"

"It came from my grandmother. She was killed," I murmured.

"Oh, I'm so sorry," he said. I felt his fingertips brush my elbow; like he wanted to offer a reas-suring touch, but also understood we were strangers.

"Thanks. It's just a lot to take in. Magic and family gifts. I just want to make her proud, you know?"

"I'm sure you will. Come on, we better get this upstairs before the orientation. Don't want to miss anything important."

We traipsed up two more flights of stairs and finally found my room. There was a second set of bags on the bed closest to the door. I'd have to get to know my roommate later. I set my belongings down on the other bed.

"Thanks again for the help," I said to Lee as he hung back just out of the doorway. Maybe he thought he might be struck down if he set foot in the room. Then again, it was entirely possible he would be.

I pulled the door shut, locked it with my key, and waited for him to ensure his belongings had arrived in his room before we descended the stairs and followed the placards directing new students to the auditorium. The new class hadn't seemed large when we'd been milling around outside, but crammed in together, there had to be at least fifty of us. Lee and I found seats in the back.

"So, the rumor goes that O'Sullivan took over the job as Dean of Students almost right after graduating," Lee whispered.

"Guess he must have been really good at the job," I answered as the man stepped up to a podium.

"Good morning, everyone. I want to welcome you to your first term here at Kismet Academy. For those who want to put a face to the name, I am Dr. Ronan O'Sullivan, Dean of Students." His voice echoed in the space even without the aid of a microphone. It must have been some form of magic I didn't understand. "Before we let you disperse to get your course schedules and get to know your fellow classmates, I wanted to impart the academy's rules on you all. First, attendance of class is a mandatory part of your study. Just because you were guaranteed a space here does not mean you do not need to show up for lessons. Miss too many classes and you will not be permitted to return next term." He glanced down at something in his hand. "Respect your fellow students, even if they may come from a different background than yourself. Your magics are unique, but that doesn't mean you can't learn from one another."

"No one cares about the hippy crap," a male voice said from the row in front of us.

"And perhaps most importantly, for your safety, the far edge of the grounds beyond the pond are strictly off limits."

"Why?" a chorus of voices rang out.

"Unfortunately, some years ago, a nasty curse befell part of the grounds that we have been unable to remove. So, for your safety, again, I will remind you to stay away."

"My father told me that when he was here, there were stories that some third year students got into some really dangerous magic and someone died,"

Lee said as O'Sullivan clapped his hands to dismiss us.

"No way, it was some crazy sex shit," the guy who'd made the hippy comment said, turning to look at us. "I heard that if you go out that way, you're going to end up horny as hell. Maybe someone died from screwing too much."

"That's awful that someone died. But shouldn't we just heed the warning?" I noted and stood up.

"Well, whether it was sex or dark magic, if someone died out there and it's been cursed for that long, they can't honestly believe people are going to stay away. It's like telling people not to think about pink elephants," Lee replied.

The topic of conversation was beginning to make me uncomfortable. "I'm going to head back and see what courses I've got. I'll see you around," I said and offered a small wave before departing the auditorium. I climbed up the six flights of stairs and returned to my dorm to find the door unlocked and ajar. My roommate, whoever she was, had beaten me back. I didn't want to startle her, so I made a show of knocking.

"Hi, uh, it's your roommate, just coming in," I said.

A lanky girl with olive skin and raven black hair

twisted into a bun at the nape of her neck stood at the desk on what had become my side of the room by default. "Oh, I didn't think you'd be back for a while," she said.

"I'm Mae Lin," I said, offering a hand.

She looked at me down the length of her angular nose. "Lani." She didn't shake my hand. "I'm taking this desk."

"Oh, I thought you'd taken that side," I said, pointing to her belongings.

"Changed my mind."

Good thing I hadn't unpacked yet. "Oh, okay."

I pulled my bags to the other side of the room and watched Lani as she studied what I assumed was her course schedule. I found mine on the other desk. First thing in morning I had Introduction to Magics followed by something called Wisher 101. There was a Fundamental Magics course on Wednesday afternoons. Then an Introductory Alchemy course on Thursday mornings.

"Have we got anything together?" I called, trying to see what her schedule entailed.

"There's no way they'd put me in any of the newbie classes," she answered with a smirk. She glanced at her paper and frowned. "I can't believe they stuck me in Intro Alchemy."

I wanted to say that at least we would be in it together, but I did not get the warmest feeling from my new dorm mate. I didn't want to be rude and assume she was djinn, but I was curious to see what someone who knew about their power could do.

"You're staring," she said in an irritated tone.

"Sorry, I was just wondering … what sort of powers you've got. Like you said, I've got all intro courses. I'm so new at this."

She gave an exaggerated eye roll and waved one hand. A travel mug materialized on the desk beside her. I could smell the strong scent of hazelnut coffee.

"I wi—" She was across the room, clamping her hand over my mouth before I could finish speaking.

"How stupid are you? Jeez. You have to at least know the basic rule."

I shook my head with her hand still covering my mouth. "Never say those two words."

"Wha' wors," I mouthed around her hand.

She pulled her fingers away long enough to scribble something on a spare piece of paper and thrust it at me. She'd written the words 'I wish.' I didn't have time to ask her why not before she'd left the room and me behind. She was right, I had a lot to learn and I was eager to get started. As I stared out the window, I could just make out the edge of the pond on the grounds.

'Mae Lin ... find me.'

That same voice called to me, stronger than it had on my first visit. I found myself halfway down the first set of stairs before my brain had caught up with my body. I forced myself to stop, gripping the banister tight to halt any forward momentum. I took several steadying breaths before I allowed myself to move down the stairs in search of the mess hall. Food and meeting my classmates would be a good distraction from the strange voice beckoning me where I suspected I shouldn't go. It wasn't a permanent fix, but it would do. For now.

CHAPTER FOUR

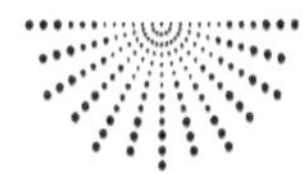

I fought the draw of the voice calling to me overnight and woke early, pulling on the uniform that still felt like it belonged in a preparatory school. Lani was nowhere to be seen. Even so, her bed was neatly made. For a moment, I wondered if she'd been able to make it using magic. That realization put a spring in my step as I made my way back down to the mess hall for breakfast. I had been so focused on just getting to the academy that I hadn't considered all of the cool things a person could do with magic.

The room was bustling even as the clock read 7:30. I hadn't seen much of the older students the day before, but they took up nearly half of the available space in the mess hall now. I spotted a few semi-familiar faces among the throngs of people standing in line at the buffet-style serving stations. My stomach rumbled with an odd mixture of hunger and anxiety. I had thought first-day-of-school jitters disappeared when I'd made it past the first grade. Apparently, being surrounded by people with magical abilities and not having a clue how to use my own brought me back to that sense of unfamiliarity and otherness.

"Hey," Lee's voice called above the din of the room.

I spotted him at a half-empty table in the corner and gave him a wave. I motioned to the line of food and he offered a thumb's up in response before I got in line. Ten minutes later, thanks to the choosiest guy I'd ever seen browsing the bagels, I sat down across from the one person I could sort of call a friend in this place.

"I wasn't expecting it to be so busy this early," I said.

"Most classes start by eight. At least that's what I've heard," he answered around a bite of strawberry jam-laden toast.

"I've got Introduction to Magics first thing," I told him. "My roommate is unhappy we've got Intro Alchemy together."

"Why is she upset about that?"

"I think she thinks she's above needing the basic courses."

"Well, we'll probably see each other in Wisher 101 later today."

I smiled at the realization that he was probably right. "At least I'll know someone."

"You really don't know much about your powers," he said.

"I guess my grandmother assumed she would pass them on to my father when the time came."

Even though her words had told me the complete opposite, I still couldn't accept that this power, whatever it was, had been meant for me all along. If that had been the case, why hadn't she prepared me for it? Now there was no one to answer those lingering questions.

Across the room, I spotted a young woman sitting by herself. She sported dark-red hair and kept glaring at a table full of guys who were leering at her. One even made a half-hearted attempt to throw a wadded-up napkin in her direction. I couldn't explain why, but I felt drawn to her. Before I had a chance to invite her to join us, a loud bell tolled throughout the room.

"Guess that means it's time to let the learning begin," Lee said with a smirk.

I followed his lead, dumped my food tray by the door, and headed to the second floor that housed several hallways lined with classrooms. The room denoted as '205' had a small sign reading Introduction to Magics beneath the number.

"I'll see you next class," Lee said with a little wave before heading across the hall.

I took a steadying breath before entering Room 205. A heavy-set man sat behind the desk reading a book. There were only about ten seats in the room and two long tables. I settled in a middle seat and pulled out a notebook and pen, ready to absorb the information about to be imparted. The room was quiet, save for the subtle flutter of the pages of the man's book turning. As time ticked by with us the only inhabitants of the room, my anxiety ratcheted up a notch. *Am I the only one stupid enough to need this class?*

The door opened and a couple of other students made their way in to find seats. By the time the man at the front of the room set his book aside, we'd risen in numbers to five students. To my relief, I wasn't the only person who looked like me in the group. In fact, all three groups were represented.

The red-haired girl from the mess hall sat in the back, slouching in her chair as if to make herself smaller.

"Right, this is Introduction to Magics," the man said in a booming bass tone. "So please make sure you're in the right class." He paused for a moment and when no one got up and left, he continued. "I'm Dr. Seamus Hennessey. You can call me Dr. H."

He moved to lean against the front of his desk, in what I'm sure he thought was a casual posture. One that would make us feel at ease in his presence. "Now, this isn't going to be a very intensive course. Assuming you pay attention and do the reading, you'll pass with no issues."

"I heard this is only a semester-long course," a young woman with a light soprano voice said from the front of the room.

"Aye, so let's get started, shall we?" He pushed off the desk and moved to the barren white board at the front of the room.

I sat up; pen poised to begin taking notes as he scribbled a few things on the board in an almost illegible script. I squinted at the words, but still couldn't make out much except for two words which he'd taken care to write large.

I Wish.

He drew a giant circle around and then a line through the words and tapped it with the back end of the marker. "First thing you need to get into your heads, you never say these two words followed by anything."

One of the only guys in the class, sitting beside me, raised a hand. "Why not?"

Dr. Hennessey let out a prolonged sigh of exasperation. "Because the act of wishing is powerful. If you aren't precise in your wording and you don't consider all of the potential consequences, what you think is a simple request gets tangled up with string you can't undo."

That explained why Lani had been so adamant about shutting me up yesterday. If I'd finished my sentence about wishing I could have done something as cool as she'd demonstrated, but there was no telling what I might have been stuck with. Or how it might have affected her. Not knowing that simple rule had made me feel foolish. Even if the other four students in my class didn't know it, either.

"Now, as this is the first day, I didn't expect you lot to have prepared anything," Hennessey said and snapped his fingers. Thick textbooks materialized in front of each of us. "As we only meet once per week, you'll be required to complete assigned readings before our next lesson and be prepared to discuss the material. Your other lessons may be more physically intensive, but building a foundation in this class will be just as important."

I stowed the book in my bag, making note of the page numbers he'd scrawled on the board for the next lesson. A clock I hadn't noticed chimed from the front of the room and Hennessey made a sweeping gesture toward the door. "Right, out you get."

I took my time gathering myself until I was the last person in the room with Dr. Hennessey. He eyed me as he waved a hand and the text he'd written disappeared, except for the assignment.

"Oh, I've written it down already," I said when our gazes met.

He nodded and the text disappeared. "You aren't going to be the silent type in my class, I hope," he said.

"No, sir. At least, I don't plan to be. I just … I feel like everyone else at least knows something about magic and I'm absolutely clueless."

"You'll catch up. It's not as steep a learning curve as people like to pretend. Just put in the work, and you'll be fine, Ms. Zhou."

"Thank you."

"Now, go on. You don't want to be late for your next class."

I checked my schedule and the tension that had crept into my shoulders relaxed. My next class was only two doors down. I walked in to find about twenty students in the room. I found a seat next to Lee and tapped him on the shoulder.

"How was your first class?" I asked.

"Not bad. Didn't do much except go over the syllabus. You?"

"Same. Well, and Dr. H made sure we all knew the first rule."

"Never say the magic words," he repeated and I couldn't help but smile.

Before I could speak, the door opened and Dr. Shen walked in. A hush fell over the room as she took up residence behind a lectern at the front of the room. "Good morning, everyone. As you may recall, my name is Dr. Shen. I will be your teacher for Wisher 101."

Her voice was soft and I leaned forward in my chair to make sure I didn't miss anything she had to say. I wasn't the only one paying close attention when next she spoke.

"You are going to find that much of what you learn here is universal. Regardless of where your magic comes from, or how it manifests, it follows certain constants. My colleagues will help guide you through those broader lessons. Our classes together this year, will focus on your unique abilities as wishers. And make no mistake, you may all come from similar bloodlines, but no two wishers' magic operates the same. We will explore what triggers your particular gifts and how to channel that power."

She clapped her hands and stepped out from behind the lectern. "In fact, I want to do a little exercise with everyone. I know it's still early, but I want to get your blood flowing. Stand up."

I was on my feet before everyone else, earning a few annoyed looks from the girls on the other side of the classroom. I watched the way Dr. Shen held her head high, her shoulders relaxed, and her hands loose at her sides. I did my best to mirror her stance.

"I want you all to close your eyes and feel the weight of your body. Just feel yourself standing there."

"I thought we were supposed to be learning how to do magic, not yoga," one of the girls snickered.

"If you aren't in tune with your body, you aren't going to be able to understand the signals it sends you on how to use your magic," Shen replied calmly.

I did as she'd instructed, focusing on my breath

and the way my body felt standing there between the desk and the chair. The pressure of the edge of the chair was constant against the backs of my knees. My fingertips brushed the rough edge of the desk in front of me and my neck muscles tensed at holding my head straight.

"Keep breathing," Shen called.

The sounds of the classroom started to melt away as I focused on my breathing. Each inhale expanded my chest and shoulders, making me feel somehow lighter each time.

"Now, I want you to feel the air around you. Feel the current that runs through it."

On cue, the air around me grew thick like I was trying to move in wet sand. It tugged on me, trying to weigh me down. I continued breathing and moment by moment that dragging feeling lightened. Like whatever was charged in the air had just wanted to let me know it was there long enough to tempt me to want to know more. I felt my fingers extend in a grasping motion, as if I could catch this unseen force, but stopped short when a loud 'crack' broke my concentration.

"Don't move," Shen's voice was firm.

My eyes flew open to reveal one of the girls who'd given me annoyed looks earlier had somehow managed to ignite the desk in front of her. I expected Shen to reach for a fire extinguisher. Instead, she waved her hands in a fanning motion and a gust of cool air whipped through the room followed by a tiny rain cloud. A heavy rain pummeled the flames, putting them out instantly. The girl scooted back as far as she could, head bowed in embarrassment.

"And that is why you must listen to the instructions I give. Trying to access or harness that power without the proper training or safeguards in place is dangerous," Shen said and produced a towel from midair, wiping down the desk. The wood wasn't even charred.

"Now, everyone, please try again. But this time, once you feel the energy around you, I want you to just let it wrap around you. Learn what it feels like when you're connected to it. But do not attempt to act with it." Her last words were sharp.

I tried to block out the mishap with my classmate and focused on the task at hand, but whatever magic I'd felt before wouldn't come this time. Instead, when I closed my eyes and focused on the feeling of my body taking up space, I felt weightless. I tried to press my legs against the chair to ground myself, but I was drifting and then the voice called my name.

Mae Lin ... please, find me ...

I could swear I felt a hand wrap around my wrist, tugging on my hand in an effort to guide me. When my eyes opened again, I found myself holding my right wrist in my left hand. Heat bloomed in my cheeks as I realized it had been my own touch I'd felt. Mercifully, no one seemed to have noticed.

Deep down, I knew I couldn't ignore the call. Maybe, if I could find whatever it was that kept reaching out for me, it would stop. I'd come here to learn about my power so I could find my grandmother's killer and bring him to justice. I was convinced he'd somehow used magic to hurt her.

But following the voice in the middle of the day seemed foolish. I suspected my search would take me to the off-limits portion of the grounds and I didn't need to make that trek in broad daylight. I wanted the calling to stop, but I wasn't stupid enough to want to get caught doing it. So, I just had to hope it would call me again tonight when I could more easily sneak away.

"Alright everyone, I want you to practice connecting to the feeling of the magic around you before our next lesson. Be mindful you don't try to use it," Shen called, disrupting my thoughts.

My first day was not shaping up at all how I'd

expected. I felt far more alone than I realized. Though as I made my way out of the classroom and back up to the dorms, I vowed to find where I belonged. I could see at least now that I had power inside of me and I owed it to myself to see what I was capable of.

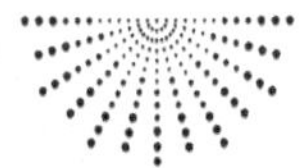

CHAPTER FIVE

Focusing on anything but my illicit campus exploration was impossible as the afternoon dragged on. I tried doing the breathing exercise Dr. Shen had shown us, hoping it would trigger the voice to call to me again. Only nothing happened.

I'd been holed up in the dorm for almost two hours when the door opened and Lani bounced in. I hadn't seen her all day and she didn't even register my presence when she sat down at her desk.

"How was your first day?" I set my book aside, hoping the slightly frosty introduction we'd had could be attributed to the fact we didn't know each other.

She turned in her chair and glared at me. "Just

because we have to share the same room, doesn't mean we have to actually talk to each other."

"Sorry, I was just trying to be nice," I answered, taken aback by her tone.

"Well, I didn't ask you to be nice. I didn't ask for a roommate at all," she griped. "I think it would be better if you found somewhere else to study. Your newbie energy is ruining my focus."

I opened my mouth to argue that I had every right to be in the room too except stopped short. Fighting with her was going to get me nowhere. Besides, it gave me an excuse to go snooping. I shouldered my bag and retreated back into the hallway. I didn't really want to bring my books with me where I was going, but I needed her to think I was actually heading to the library to study.

Of course, that assumed I could actually find the library in the first place. It seemed a decent place to store my things and I did need to know where it was. I started down the stairs, stopping on the landing of each floor and peering down the long hallways, but nothing stood out. I reached the third floor and spotted Dr. Hennessey in conversation with a young woman with cornrows. I approached them, hanging back so as not to interrupt their conversation. Hennessey spotted me, whispered something to the woman and closed the distance between us.

"Evening Ms. Zhou. You look a little turned around."

It wasn't a deception if it was the truth. "A little. I was looking for the library. I wanted some quiet to do some reading and I can't remember where it is."

He hooked a thumb over his shoulder down the hallway. "All the way at the end."

"Thanks."

He gave me a brief nod before turning back to his prior conversation. I half-expected the library to be abuzz with students trying to get their studying in early, but the space was eerily quiet. An older man sat at the desk marked 'Reference' reading a book. I scanned the rows of shelves and tables lining the far wall. I wound my way through the stacks until I found a secluded space out of the line of sight of the librarian and other students. I stashed my bag beneath a table and sunk into a chair.

Now that I'd found this place, I needed to figure out how I was going to make it down to the first floor and outside without being seen. I was certain if I had any idea how magic worked, I could just teleport myself or turn myself invisible. Except I had none of those skills. I'd never been the type of kid to sneak out after curfew growing up.

"Think Mae Lin," I grumbled at myself.

The voice had been quiet since this morning's lesson. Though the time before when I'd heard it, my body had responded before my brain had caught up. If I could just find it again, maybe it would lead me there and whatever connection we shared would be enough to hide me from prying eyes.

I got to my feet and closed my eyes. I took slow, even breaths and felt the weight of the world around me and my body's place in it, just as Dr. Shen had instructed. That feeling of dragging through wet sand returned and I relaxed a little. At least this tenuous connection to magic hadn't been a fluke in the classroom.

"Come on, help me out."

'Come find me ...'

I opened my eyes just enough to see my surroundings. I crept along the far wall to a back exit near a stairwell that only led down to the first floor. I moved with quick steps to the main floor and out a side entrance I had no reason to know existed. It brought me out closer to the far edge of the pond. I managed to halt my forward momentum long enough to take in the grounds from this angle. The pond stretched further than I'd originally thought in all directions. The more I tried to navigate around it, the wider it seemed to grow.

They really don't want people going beyond here.

Progress remained slow, but steady. Above me, the sky darkened to navy and purple hues. The sun disappeared completely by the time I made it around the circumference of the pond and made it to a large limestone structure. My skin crawled the moment I touched the front door. This place felt *wrong*. Almost the same way the restaurant had felt the day *Nai-Nai* was killed. The rational part of me wanted to retreat. I wasn't equipped yet to handle whatever lay within these walls. Yet, standing here the pull of the voice intensified. I could feel phantom fingers trying to wrap around my wrists to tug me closer.

I pushed down my fear and slipped through the opening in the entryway. The interior smelled damp and musty, and I couldn't stop myself from coughing. I clamped a hand over my mouth the second the sound came out as the realization dawned on me that if this place was supposed to be off-limits, the front door shouldn't have been open.

I'd also expected the space to be unlit, yet there was a soft golden glow emanating from further inside the structure. I was definitely not alone here. I opened my mouth to call out, but thought better of it. I had no idea who or what had been calling to me. I was fairly certain whatever the answer, it wasn't something I should go rushing into unprepared. I took a hesitant step forward and froze.

A sharp buzzing sound pulled my attention to the lefthand side of the space. Something metallic whizzed by me, clipping my arm before embedding into the stone behind me with a firm 'crack.'

"I'm sorry," I blurted.

"Who the hell are you?" a low female voice demanded.

Definitely not the same person who'd guided me here. From the depths of the cramped space, the same red-haired girl from Intro to Magics appeared. She held a collection of sharp-looking weapons in her hands. The tension in her shoulders dipped a fraction.

"They send you to find me?" her tone carried an edge as sharp as her weapons.

"Who?" I blinked at her. "No one sent me. I, uh, sort of came looking for this place on my own. I had no idea anyone would be here."

She pushed her way past me and peered out the still-open doorway. "You sure you weren't followed?"

"I don't think so," I answered, pressing the tip of my right index finger to the cut in my blazer. My fingertip came away red with blood and I winced as the pain caught up to me. "Ow."

The girl turned back to look at me, sliding the cache of weapons into a pouch on her hip. "Shit, sorry I didn't think I hit you. I really thought you were someone else."

"I'll be fine," I said, keeping pressure on the cut.

"I'm Siobhan, by the way," she said, holding out a hand.

I shook it awkwardly with my left. "Mae Lin."

"You were in Intro the Magics," she noted.

"I honestly thought I was going to be the only one in there," I admitted. "I didn't even know what was happening when my grandmother passed the magic to me."

"That's rough. Was it sudden?"

"She was murdered."

"Bloody hell, I'm sorry."

"I was hoping coming here would help me figure out how to use these powers, so I can find the person responsible and bring them to justice."

"Well, I doubt you'll get much out of boring Dr. H's lectures." Siobhan snickered.

"I thought it was useful."

"Oh, come on, everyone knows the golden rule."

I averted my gaze and she let out a little choked sound I interpreted as embarrassment. I really was the most inexperienced person on this campus not to know that you shouldn't ever say I wish. Had I just gotten lucky with Dr. O'Sullivan showing up when I'd uttered those words two weeks ago?

"I may have said it once. It's how I found out about the academy," I mumbled.

"Lucky it didn't result in something catastrophic," she noted.

"Yeah." After a moment, I looked up at her again. "Can I ask what you were doing in here? And why you thought whoever might be coming in warranted attacking?"

Her hand twitched, brushing the clasp on the pouch at her hip. "It's a bit complicated. But I just wanted some space and privacy. Lot of the blokes in class aren't fond of me."

"They don't even know you," I scoffed. Not that I could claim to know her better.

"Leprechauns are a tight community. I've known most of them since I was a kid," she replied. "And they just aren't fond of me."

The way she pressed her lips into a tight line that made them almost disappear into the rest of her face suggested there was more to the story than she was willing to share. And why should she? I was a total stranger.

"Where'd you get those?" I gestured to the weapon still sticking out of the wall. I took a step closer to examine it. From this close up I could see it was a throwing star.

She perked up. "Made them myself. Bit of leprechaun gold, really durable and it never loses its edge."

"Well, I'm sorry I interrupted your solitude."

"We've established why I am in here. What about you? No offense, but you don't seem the type to go seeking out creepy crypts."

Crypt?

"Uh, it's going to sound crazy, but I heard someone calling me. Whatever it was, it brought me here" I explained. "And what makes you think this is a crypt?"

She gestured to the walls. I took a step closer and saw little silver plaques with names and dates, some going back hundreds of years. A shiver danced down my spine at the realization something magical had lured me to a crypt full of dead bodies. My hand slipped off my arm, letting up on the pressure on the cut. I felt a droplet of blood slip down my fingertip and land with an audible 'plop' on the floor.

We weren't supposed to be here and leaving behind evidence was a foolish move. I bent to try and use the sleeve of my blazer to wipe it up when the droplet vibrated and disappeared into the cracks in the floor. The stone beneath my feet shook, sending me stumbling backwards into Siobhan.

"What the hell was that?" she demanded.

"I don't know," I answered, my throat going dry.

'Mae Lin. Please, help.'

The voice was stronger, more insistent than it had been before. My head whipped around, trying to place the direction of the sound. Yet it didn't appear to have come from anywhere in particular.

"Did you hear that?"

"You mean the walls about collapse in on us?" she answered, yanking the weapon she'd thrown at me from the wall.

I didn't correct her as we scrambled out of the crypt, slamming the door shut with our combined weight. We both took off at a run, darting around the edge of the pond. It had to be adrenaline causing us to reach the far side in half the time it had taken to make the reverse trip.

"You have any idea why that place just suddenly

decided to have its own little earthquake?" Siobhan demanded.

"No," I answered, trying to catch my breath. "But something is off in there. I heard whatever was calling to me again. It was stronger this time."

"You do know that hearing voices is not generally a good sign, whether you've got magic or not."

I couldn't help glaring at her. "I know that. And I'm not crazy." At least I didn't think so.

High above us, a quarter moon cast weak light through the inky darkness. It didn't seem possible we'd been in there long enough for the sun to completely vanish from the sky. We walked together in silence back to the main building. The whole ordeal had spiked my stress response, but I was crashing hard now. I just wanted to crawl into bed and sleep, but my belongings were still in the library.

"You wouldn't happen to know how late the library's open?" I whispered as we approached the side entrance I'd exited earlier.

"Not this late."

I'd have to risk getting up early to retrieve my belongings and hope no one had reported the unattended bag in the meantime. "Well, guess I'll see you in class," I offered.

"Yeah. See you 'round. And uh, how about we keep this whole thing between us?"

"Absolutely."

Siobhan and I parted ways on the fifth floor, and I crept into my room. Lani snored softly in her bed. I peeled off my blazer and winced at the cut on my arm. I slipped into the communal bathroom and breathed a sigh of relief when I found basic first aid supplies under the sink. It would have been easier with a second pair of hands, but I managed to disinfect and wrap the wound.

Settling beneath the covers ten minutes later, I focused on my heart rate. Even all this time later, it still thumped double time in my chest. I took deep breaths, hoping it would settle enough to let me sleep. I didn't know what tonight's adventure meant, but I knew it was just the beginning.

CHAPTER SIX

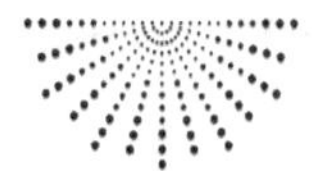

I didn't think it was possible for my entire body to ache as I dragged myself out of bed the next morning. Yet it felt as if Siobhan's throwing star had hit me all over. Thankfully, the bandage from the night before had held and blended in enough with my blouse to not be noticeable.

The stairwell was empty as I made my way to the third floor and into the library. The clock above the reference desk read six-forty. Apparently not even the librarian was up this early. I retraced my steps to the back of space to the table I'd briefly occupied yesterday evening. My heart skipped a beat when I peered beneath the table to find it empty. Someone had turned it in.

"Looking for something?" a high male voice called from behind me.

I spun on my heel to find the librarian standing there between the stacks holding my bag in one hand. "Oh, uh, yes. That's mine."

He eyed me, like he couldn't decide whether to trust me or not. "It's generally frowned upon to leave your belongings overnight."

"I know. I'm sorry. It was a mistake. I was so busy studying, I guess I forgot some of my things when I left yesterday," I lied. A knot tightened in my stomach as I waited for him to make a decision on whether he believed me.

"Don't let it happen again," he sighed and held my bag by the strap.

Snatching it out of his hands, I made a beeline down to the mess hall and claimed a table near the door. I grabbed coffee and a fresh made breakfast sandwich and sat down, skimming through the syllabus for Intro to Magics. It made me anxious, not having done any reading yet, even though our next class wasn't until next week.

"How's the arm?" Siobhan's voice was hushed as she slid into the seat across from me, her weight making the faux vinyl squeak.

"It's fine," I replied, looking up from the paper and book spread out on the table in front of me.

She snatched a sliver of bacon from my plate. "You're probably going to learn more and faster from the practical classes," she noted.

"I'm sure there's stuff I can't learn that way," I replied.

"So, what do you think called you there?" She whispered, leaning in close to avoid eavesdroppers. Even though we were the only two people in the room.

"I don't know exactly. Whatever it is, it started when I came to tour the campus with Dr. O'Sullivan." I pushed my plate away. "I've heard the rumors about that place. Someone died there. There has to be a reason it's off limits."

"I call bullshit," she answered.

"Why?"

"Don't get me wrong, I think something really messed up went down there, but if someone did die, you better believe the faculty would have gotten rid of whatever had led to a death."

"Maybe you're right. I know that there has to be a reason this is happening, especially when I'm trying to get in touch with my magic. I don't want to believe it's malevolent, but maybe I'm just being naïve?"

Siobhan didn't answer. Instead, she darted from her seat and disappeared from the room. I turned, craning my neck to see what had made her flee. I spotted Lee in conversation with a few red-haired guys, who I was beginning to assume were leprechauns. Were they the ones she'd been expecting to follow her last night?

Overhead, the bell tolled signaling the start of morning classes. I made my way up to the second floor for my morning class, surprised to see Dr. O'Sullivan seated behind the desk at the front of the room. He caught me staring and offered up a smile.

"Just because I'm Dean of Students doesn't mean I don't still teach," he offered.

"Of course," I replied, taking a seat in the middle of the room.

I watched as more students filtered in. This room was a large lecture hall, able to accommodate perhaps half of our class. To my surprise, Lani strode in. She caught sight of me and she stiffened. Apparently, she was unhappy we shared two classes. She approached O'Sullivan at the front of the room.

"Really, Dr. O'Sullivan, I thought our schedules

weren't supposed to change after the start of the semester. I think this is a mistake."

O'Sullivan arched a brow. "If your schedule says to be here, then take a seat." He leaned in as if to whisper something to her, but his voice carried. "And I would suggest you not air your grievances about class assignments in front of everyone."

She let out an audible huff and sat down at the back of the room. Lee, seated beside me, couldn't hide a snicker.

"She thinks because her family donates to the school, she deserves special treatment."

Lani hadn't mentioned anything like that to me, but it was clear she thought she was better than everyone else here. It would also explain why she thought she could boss me around in our dorm. She probably had expected to get her own room, because of her family's status.

"Right, now that we've all settled in, let's begin," O'Sullivan said, standing up from behind his desk. "Today, we will begin exploring the origins of magic as we understand it."

O'Sullivan snapped his fingers and a projector turned on overhead, displaying a slideshow on the whiteboard at the front of the room. I tried to focus on his words as he began to lecture.

"Centuries ago, you all would be receiving your education directly from your families, only learning your bloodline's gifts." He pointed to a few of the red-headed students in class. "Leprechauns would pass down the skill of working with gold and teleportation via rainbow."

He spun and gave a flourish-filled gesture toward Lani. It was clearly a jab at her snootiness and I couldn't keep myself from smirking to myself. "Djinn passed on the secrets to wish granting and learning to weave the wording just so ..." He turned and looked directly at me. "And wishers would pass along the magic used to bestow futures on those around them."

"He's oversimplifying it," Lee whispered, nudging me in the arm.

I winced, instinctively pressing my hand to the wound and he arched a brow. "What's wrong?"

"Nothing," I lied, trying to turn back to O'Sullivan's presentation. Everyone else might have a basic understanding of where they came from, but I had to learn from scratch. I needed the information he was imparting.

"You can tell me," Lee prodded.

"Later. I'm trying to take notes," I muttered.

"Now, each bloodline has great power and skill in their own right," O'Sullivan continued. "But we finally figured out that there were benefits to sharing our gifts with each other. To cross-pollenate ideas and skills to provide a more cohesive community."

The projector clicked and a new image of three people, each putting off a different colored aura, appeared on the whiteboard. I recognized the figures as the ones from the front gates. Without him having to say the words, I understood they were the founders of the academy.

"Now, you're going to have to learn about these fascinating dead folks this term," O'Sullivan said with a chuckle. "But I promise they've got some fun little secrets in their histories to be discovered."

"This is so stupid," Lani protested loudly.

"Now, just because we come from different backgrounds doesn't mean we're that different. You are going to pair off and share some information about yourselves. The point of this exercise is to break down the assumptions we have about each other."

I started to turn toward Lee when O'Sullivan added, "You are going to pair with someone who is different from you."

A chorus of groans went up around the room. I cast Lee an apologetic look before I stood with my notebooks and went in search of a partner. I knew there was very little chance I wanted to be paired with Lani if given a choice.

"You looking for a partner?" a dark-haired guy with an elaborate forearm tattoo and British accent said.

I sat down beside him, grateful to be rescued. "Yeah, thanks."

"I'm Basil," he said, his accent becoming more pronounced as he said his name.

"Mae Lin. Nice to meet you."

He glanced over his shoulder at Lani as she continued to glare at everyone around her. Several people had tried to cram in around her. Basil let out a snort. "Entitled princess."

"You don't have to live with her," I sighed.

"We're not all like her," he offered.

"I didn't think you were," I replied.

"So, tell me something about yourself," he said, leaning back in his chair and crossing his arms over his chest. The tattoo—which I now realized was a serpent undulated as he flexed his muscles.

"Uh, well, I'm probably the most inexperienced

person on campus. I didn't even realize what was happening with I got my powers."

"You'll catch up. A lot of the stuff is pretty much common sense and intuition. The magic wants to be used and we're hardwired to be its conduit. A little discipline and any of us could be running this place or more."

"So, you've always had your powers?"

"Yeah. It's kind of weird to me to think about not having powers until someone else passes them on. I mean, all we get sometimes is a family obligation."

"You mean like being bound to a master?" I hated myself for saying it.

Basil wasn't offended. He laughed. "Not in ages. But some families once they gained freedom did make promises to serve and protect communities. The last three generations of my family have all been police."

"Guessing you'll be the fourth?"

"I know that's what they want me to be."

"But you want to do something else. There has to be another way for you to serve the community in a way that makes you happy."

"What about you? Wishers always seem so, I don't know, isolated. Just sitting in their towers casting into the future."

I closed my eyes and tried to picture Nai-Nai doing that. It hadn't seemed like she was isolated from the rest of us. She had always made a point to go out and socialize with the people who came to the restaurant. She made time for her family.

"It wasn't like that, at least not for my family. Sure, we own a restaurant, and I see now that my grandmother was doling out fortunes to people with magic, but she wasn't lonely. We were a big part of our community. People came to us, because they trusted her guidance."

Basil glanced toward the front of the room. "I suppose we've just completed his assignment, then. Learned something new about each other. Broken down some stereotypes."

"Seems so. Thanks again for being my partner. I was honestly worried no one was going to want to talk to me. Seeing as I'm so new to this."

Basil shrugged. "People can be arseholes about stupid things. And you shouldn't let what you think their opinion is of you color your judgment. You've got every right to be here. So, own that space." As he spoke his final words, I could swear the serpent on his arm hovered off his skin and flicked its tongue at me.

"Did that just *move*?" I rasped.

Basil swatted at his arm and the tattoo settled back onto his skin. "Sorry, she gets a little excited sometimes."

"Is that djinn magic?" I felt stupid for asking.

"Cool, huh?" he grinned and lowered his voice. "Most people think it's an illusion, but she's actually my familiar."

"Do all djinn have those?" I tried to soak up everything he was telling me.

"Not everyone. Some have more of an affinity for bonding with a creature. Agnes has been with me since I was eight."

I tried to imagine an eight-year-old with a tattoo of a giant serpent and had to cover my mouth to stop from snickering out loud. Basil smiled at me, as if he could read my mind.

The projector clicked off overhead and O'Sullivan stood. "All right, that's all for today. I've assigned some reading for next lesson."

I retrieved my bag with the rest of my books and left the classroom behind. My discussion with Basil had been illuminating. There was still so much I wanted to know about this world.

"Learn anything?" Lee's voice floated to me from a few paces behind me.

"I did actually," I answered as he fell into step beside me.

"So, want to tell me about what happened with your arm?"

"It's embarrassing, really," I said, hoping he'd drop it.

"Were you trying to do magic?" he pressed.

"No. I, uh … just had a run in with the wrong end of a throwing star."

He wheeled on me and blocked my path forward. "You what? Someone attacked you. Did you report it to O'Sullivan?"

His hands hovered a half-inch above my upper arms, like he wanted to grab me, but didn't want to hurt me. "Really, I'm fine. No one attacked me. It was just a misunderstanding."

I spotted Siobhan down the hallway. "Siobhan is nice. At least I think she is. Anyway, that's not the weirdest thing that happened last night."

"What could be weirder than that?'

I urged him toward an alcove and leaned in close. "We were in the crypt and this voice called to me. And then the whole place shook like it was going to collapse."

He pulled his wire-rim glasses off and rubbed the bridge of his nose. "What would possess you to go near that place? You heard O'Sullivan say it was off limits. Are you trying to get kicked out?"

"Calm down. We didn't get caught and yes, I heard him. But I can't explain it. It was like I was drawn there."

"Well, you aren't going back," he said in a tone that carried a note of finality.

His demeanor made me take a step back. We barely knew each other. While he seemed nice, I didn't appreciate him trying to tell me what I could or couldn't do. O'Sullivan and the other teacher at least had the clout of being faculty.

"I'm not planning to go back," I finally said.

Out of the corner of my eye I watched Siobhan making progress through the steady stream of students going the opposite direction. Lee turned to follow my gaze.

"If she's capable of hurting you by accident, I would stay away from her. You don't need that kind of trouble."

I bit my tongue to keep from lashing out at him. He didn't get to tell me who I could or couldn't associate with either. "Like I said, it was an accident. Look, I need to get going. I need to do some wisher practice exercises before my next class. I will see you later."

I left Lee standing there in the alcove. Part of me wanted to join Siobhan wherever she was going, but I did really need the practice. I didn't want to risk the librarian's ire, so I chanced a return to the dorm. Lani was mercifully absent as I settled in at my desk and began to read. I had to hope that whatever I was meant to learn here would point me in the right direction of finding my grandmother's killer.

CHAPTER SEVEN

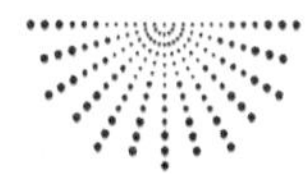

Three weeks after the start of the semester, I was finally settling into a routine of classes and avoiding Lani. It meant early mornings spent in the mess hall or outside by the pond. In some ways, it was almost peaceful to watch the sun rise each morning. The strange voice that had been calling me had disappeared. As unnerving as it was, I was beginning to miss it.

I sat in the mostly empty classroom for Introductory Alchemy, focusing on the exercises Dr. Shen had taught us that week. Much to my relief, the concentration necessary to get in touch with my magic eased with each passing day. I didn't even need to block out the world around me to feel its presence. It tingled across my skin like a soft mist. I could almost feel the magic dance along my fingertips, ready to be used. If only I knew how to direct it. Across the room, Lani sat examining her nails. I could hear her voice in the back of my head, taunting *'I can already do three times what you can.'*

The door opened and Siobhan walked in, taking her seat at the back of the room. Lee followed soon after and took up residence two seats down from me. I offered him a small wave. I hadn't talked much to Siobhan since our first encounter. She had been keeping to herself in between classes. That much I'd noticed.

"Everyone, please take your seats," Dr. Wren—a middle aged woman with a shock of white gray hair styled into a pixie cut—called from the front of the room.

Per usual, she sported safety goggles and thick gloves that went up past her elbows. Part of me believed it was just for show. In the three lessons we'd had so far, we hadn't done anything remotely close to needing protective gear. For a brief moment, I wondered if she'd made an inadvertent wish that had left her perpetually adorned with the garb. I wasn't stupid enough to ask.

My attention diverted to the board behind her, already filled with multi-colored instructions for whatever experiment she had us running today. From what I could gather, she expected us to start learning to turn base metals into gold. I was pretty sure that was impossible even with magic. Out of the corner of my eye, I spotted Siobhan sit up a little straighter. The memory of her throwing star came to mind. I hadn't been aware enough to ask what exactly made leprechaun gold different from the normal substance. Was it alchemically created?

I wouldn't want to share that if it were my secret.

"We will be working in pairs today," Wren continued and clapped her hands twice.

My stomach dropped through the floor as my body moved through space of its own volition. I found myself sitting next to the one person I had been doing my best to avoid.

"Your task for the day is reduce the metals in front of you to their base elements and identify which compounds you would need to convert them to gold."

"You better not ruin my grade," Lani snapped.

I gritted my teeth and tried not to let her get to me. I just wanted to focus on the task at hand. "Look, why don't we each take one and see what we come up with and then compare," I suggested, putting a little distance between us.

"Fine." She snatched up what looked to be a chunk of silver, leaving me a tiny slab of something that looked a bit like tarnished copper.

Across the room, I watched Lee and Siobhan working together. She'd already taken over the equipment and appeared to be bossing him around. I laughed softly as he kept casting her annoyed looks. From the time he and I had spent together during lessons and the occasional lunch study session, I knew he, like me, was very driven by academic success on his own merits. Still, it was the most animated I'd seen the girl in all the time I'd known her.

Turning my attention back to the task at hand, I studied the lump of metal on the table. I picked it up, feeling the weight of it and held it up to my nose. It certainly smelled like copper. All around me, burners ignited as my classmates worked to distill their metals into liquid form. I hastily grabbed a dish and a burner and lit the flame. I tried to recall the melting point of copper and guessed it was far hotter than anything a normal person should be exposed to. Yet, no one else seemed worried by the experiment. Part of me worried Dr. Wren's perpetual safety gear had become so much a part of her, she forgot other people needed it. I left my metal in its little dish and wound my way to the front of the class.

"Excuse me, Dr. Wren, but we don't have any safety gear."

She looked at me, her eyes exaggerated through the goggles. "Oh, the room is warded against accidents."

"Well, I'd still feel better with some gloves and goggles. Like you've got," I replied.

"Right, right. Of course. Check the closet over there," she said, leaving me to inspect my classmate's progress.

I retreated to the closet and found safety gear, pulling out two pairs of goggles and gloves. I was close enough to overhear Siobhan and Lee's conversation.

"You're sure that's not going to hurt?" Lee's voice carried a tinge of nerves I hadn't heard before.

"How else do you think its's made?" Siobhan scoffed.

I pivoted to watch her take the metals in her hands and I heard a strange crunching sound. When she pulled her palms apart, the metal had consolidated into one lump and had taken on a golden sheen.

"How'd you do that?" I whispered as I passed by their station.

"She cheated!" Lani's voice rang out and for a moment I had no idea what she was talking about.

When I finally looked at my roommate-turned-lab-partner, I saw her pointing a shaky finger at Siobhan. Dr. Wren spun around and was at Siobhan and Lee's station in seconds. I could swear she'd tele-ported herself through several desks and chairs to get there. The instructor held her hands over the burner in front of Siobhan's space.

"Did I tell you to use magic to complete this task?"

"Well, no … but why waste time when you can just …" Siobhan began.

"The point of this exercise was *not* to create gold, but to understand how the components of different metals can be combined and enhanced to achieve that ultimate result," Wren snapped.

"I was trying to tell her that," Lee piped up.

"Get out of my classroom," Wren spat. The door slammed open like an extension of the woman's anger.

Siobhan's hand gripped the piece of gold she'd created as she stormed out of the room. I slowly retreated back to my desk to find my copper was still mostly solid. Beside my dish, I saw Lani's dish filled with liquid silver. I doubted she had gotten the temperature right for her silver to reach that consistency without a little magical assistance.

"You did the same thing," I hissed, setting the gloves and goggles down between us.

Lani let out a little huff of annoyance. "And what do you have to prove that?"

"Because no one else has even gotten close to this," I answered. "And I wouldn't put it past you to turn everyone's focus on someone else to avoid scrutiny on whatever you're doing," I answered, my own anger bubbling to the surface.

"You better watch what you say," she snarled. "Don't forget who you're talking to."

"Yeah, the girl who has to throw around the weight of her family's money to make herself feel important," I replied.

"How dare you?" Lani screeched. The liquid silver in the dish in front of her sloshed, threatening to spill over. I took a step back on instinct as color burned bright in her cheeks.

"You wouldn't know magic if it slapped you in the face, you ignorant bitch," she continued. "How pathetic are you? You didn't even know the basics before you came here. Your family must have been so ashamed of you that they didn't even tell you that. I bet you weren't even supposed to inherit magic. You don't belong here."

Logically, I knew what she was doing. We might not have spent much time together, but I'd shared enough over the last few weeks for her to know my insecurities about my place here and my naivete toward magic. It wasn't a new revelation for the rest of my classmates, either. I'd heard them whispering behind my back. But the fact that she would bring my family into this made my blood boil.

"That's enough!" Wren's voice cut through the audible rush of blood in my ears. "Both of you out, now."

I flicked the burner off and shouldered my bag. I fought the instinct to shrink away from my classmates' attention. I wasn't going to let Lani dictate how the rest of the school saw me or how I saw myself. So, I marched out of the room with my head held high. I made it past the lecture hall for O'Sullivan's class before I heard sharp footfalls behind me.

"You might think you matter, but you don't," Lani taunted. "You better not come back to the dorm."

"You don't have control over who rooms where," I reminded her.

"Do you really want to test that theory? I suggest

if you don't want to end up homeless, you get your things and get out of *my* room," she hissed.

The crackle in the air around her promised she might not have engaged in violence, but she was more than willing to let her power act as a reminder of her place here. I marched up to the sixth floor and tossed my clothes into my suitcase. I had no idea where I was going, but I started to drag my bags downstairs. I made it to the fifth floor when I heard something sink into the stone wall beside me. The throwing star wobbled before dislodging and shooting back into Siobhan's hand, bits of mortar and stone dust fell to the floor in its wake.

"You going somewhere?" she pointed at my bags.

"After you got kicked out of class, I may have called Lani out for being a hypocrite and that got us both kicked out, too. Then she threw me out of our dorm."

"She is such a bitch."

"I don't disagree. I'm sorry if my asking how you'd done what you did drew attention to you."

"It wasn't your fault. I just got excited, because it was something I knew how to do, you know? Gold is something I just *get*." After a beat, she reached out a hand for one of my suitcases. "Come on. I've got space in my room."

I didn't argue with her as she led me into the dorm and across the common area to a door marked 51. The room looked exactly like mine and Lani's save for the empty bed on the far side of the room where Siobhan set my bag.

"Don't you have a roommate?"

"Got lucky, I guess. Hope you don't snore," she answered with a small laugh.

"Not that I've been told," I answered and sunk onto the bed. Maybe I could actually get some sleep now that I didn't have to worry about not pissing off my roommate. "I really appreciate this."

"Us misfits have to stick together, right?"

"Yeah. I guess we do." I flopped down on the pillow and looked at her. "So, how did you actually turn that into gold?"

"Leprechaun DNA is just attuned to making gold. I mean, we don't literally sit at the ends of rainbows hoarding the stuff in giant pots, but we've always had an affinity for it. From what I can figure out, it's something about the secretions we give off when we're around metals."

"That's really cool."

"Not to Dr. Buzzkill," Siobhan huffed.

"I'm sure she wouldn't have been so mad if you'd tried the experiment her way first."

I realized too late that was the wrong thing to say. She'd wanted me to be on her side completely, but I could see Dr. Wren's frustration. She had wanted us to understand the why behind what we were doing before we figured out the shortcut on how to do it. Alchemy was really just science with a little bit of magic.

"I just got excited and I didn't think," Siobhan muttered.

"I'm sure there was much bigger mistakes you could have made," I assured her and rolled onto my side. "So, do you think she's always in that gear?"

Siobhan snickered and sat down on the bed on the other side of the room. "I heard some of the older students talking about how she made a bad wish twenty years ago and she doesn't even realize what happened."

"There are worse things to be stuck wearing. At least she's somewhat practical for her field."

"Your friend was pretty pissed at me," she said.

"Who, Lee? I'm sure he'll get over it. He just takes his grades seriously. I guess there are some preconceptions that ring truer than others."

"Well, at least I know I've got someone who's good at book learning for when I inevitably fall behind in the boring classes," Siobhan said and flashed me a toothy grin.

"And I've got someone to help me with the practical stuff," I replied.

Maybe today wasn't turning out to be such a terrible day after all. I'd found another friend and I was finally going to be free of Lani's overshadowing presence. And if she was telling the truth and could twist Dr. O'Sullivan's arm for getting rid of me as a roommate, that wasn't such a bad thing. Things were really starting to look up. What could possibly go wrong?

CHAPTER EIGHT

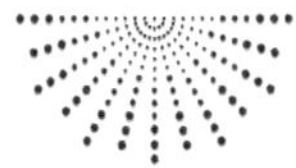

My luck lasted a whole two weeks. Just enough time for Siobhan and I to settle into a comfortable rhythm. Dr. O'Sullivan had even blessed us sharing a room, although I hadn't shared the news with Lee. He still seemed touchy about the fact she'd ruined their alchemy experiment.

"He'll get over it," she told me Saturday night.

"I know, I just hate not telling him the truth," I answered.

"I'm not stopping you," she reminded me.

There really was nothing stopping me from sharing the news with Lee. Besides, he was my only other friend here and it was becoming increasingly difficult to hide the fact I didn't live on the same floor as him anymore. Thankfully, he hadn't come looking for me for a study session.

"I'll tell him tomorrow. We're studying in the afternoon," I said, more to strengthen my own resolve than to mollify her.

"Whatever," she said through a yawn.

I settled beneath the blankets as she turned out the light. Sleep came quickly and it plunged me into what started out as a dreamless rest.

Pain pulled me from the darkness. My hands were bound at my sides, pulling my shoulder muscles taut. I could feel cold sweat clinging to all of my exposed skin as I struggled to my feet. How long had I been confined in this place? I was waiting for something ... for someone.

An image resolved from the darkness in front of me. A vague face that somehow, I knew was safe. My jaw ached from clenching for so long. It cracked as I opened my mouth to try and call to the figure slowly coalescing in front of me.

"Help ... me ..." The words were a rasp and sounded strange to my ears. Had it been that long since I'd used my voice that I didn't recognize it?

The figure's face wavered before solidifying into a beautiful young woman with dark hair and sharp brown eyes. If it were possible, relief washed over me as she took another step closer.

Suddenly, the image vanished, replaced by a reflection of myself. Dark skin and eyes I no longer recognized with sunken cheeks and hollow eyes. This is not the person I remembered being.

I opened my mouth to call for the woman again when a sharp, piercing laugh echoed around me. It jarred every nerve ending in my already tense frame, forcing a cascade of numbness to sweep from head to toe.

"You will never get out of here." The voice was booming, slamming into me from every direction.

I sat up, hair clinging to my forehead with slick sweat. I cast my eyes around, trying to find a touchstone, anything to tell me I was actually awake. I heard Siobhan's light snores from across the room and slowly sunk back against the pillow. The dream had felt so real. I tried to piece it together before it flooded my conscious memory. The figure had called for help. *Could it be the same voice that had led me to the crypt?*

No matter what story you believed, everyone seemed to agree that someone had died in that crypt. But the person I'd seen, the person I'd *been*, still seemed to be alive, if only barely.

"Siobhan, wake up," I called.

My roommate didn't respond.

I kicked off the damp bedsheets and crept across

the room, careful to keep enough distance between us that I could avoid any fists that came flying. I hadn't said anything to her. Despite that she'd woken me up more than once having very violent dreams, complete with fists swinging wildly in the air above her bed.

"Siobhan," I called, louder this time.

She moaned and rolled toward me, eyes blinking open. "What?"

"I just had a crazy dream. I can't explain it, but I think it's related to whatever led me to the crypt."

She blinked up at me twice more before forcing herself into a sitting position. "And you're telling me this …" she glanced at the clock on her night table, "at midnight, why?"

"Because I think there might actually be someone trapped there."

That got her attention. She pushed dark red curls from her face and swung her legs over the side of the bed. "What makes you think that?"

"It's a little hazy now, but it was like I was this person, trying to call out for help. It sounded like the voice I've been hearing."

"But how do you know it's in the crypt?"

"It's the only place I've felt compelled to go.

There has to be a reason. Come on, we need to check it out."

"Slow down. Not to harsh your buzz. But whether you like it or not, you don't exactly know how to use your powers yet. And it's the middle of the bloody night, and that place is off limits for a reason."

"You mean the same place you were hiding out in a month ago?" I reminded her.

"Why do I get the feeling you're calling me a coward?"

"I'm not. But, come on, wouldn't we both feel better if I had someone who could have my back?"

"If we get killed, I'm going to find a way to haunt you," she grumbled, but pulled on pants and shoes.

I'd never really been one to break the rules, but I couldn't shake the sense of despair from the dream. It had been mine and not mine all at once. If someone really was trapped down there and they were asking for my help, I had to try and free them. The halls were deserted as one would expect, but it also meant our footfalls echoed painfully with every step. My heart stopped as we reached the first floor and I heard a set of footsteps that weren't ours moving around the foyer. Siobhan and I pressed ourselves against the wall and waited as Dr. O'Sullivan moved through the space dressed in dark pants and a baggy shirt. He carried a glass of something in one hand.

I hadn't realized I'd stopped breathing until he disappeared down the hall and the hall was silent for a count of thirty. I swallowed several times to rid my mouth of the sandpaper feeling the fear of being caught had induced before we made a mad dash for the front door. I breathed a sigh of relief as the cool early morning air smacked me in the face, invigorating me.

"We need to keep moving," I urged, picking up the pace.

Unlike the first time I'd made it to the crypt, our trek around the perimeter of the pond seemed to take no time at all. We reached the heavy stone doors in record time. Unfortunately, it was then that I realized a flashlight or lamp would have come in handy.

"This is going to be harder in the dark," I muttered.

Siobhan let out an annoyed breath. "Give me a minute."

I turned and watched as she rubbed her hands together like she was packing an invisible snowball. Between her fingers pale golden light emerged, coalescing into a sphere. The golden glow I'd noticed when we'd first met made sense now.

"That's so cool." I couldn't help myself.

She gave the sphere a little toss into the air where it hovered, casting the doors in a pleasant glow. It was enough to see by and together we hauled one of the doors open enough to get inside. I shivered as we stepped inside. Being here among the dead, both gave me the creeps and yet in some small way made me feel closer to *Nai-Nai*.

"Before we go anywhere, we need a plan," Siobhan insisted, her voice echoing in the antechamber.

"Coming here was the plan," I admitted sheepishly.

"Well, you were the one who dreamt this living person in a room full of corpses, so you better figure out how we are supposed to find them," she answered.

I was about to tell her that I had no idea how to go about doing that when I stopped myself. I could figure this out. I closed my eyes and let my body relax into the ebb and flow of magic around me. Being in that semi-aware state seemed to be when whoever was here called to me the most.

I'm here. Help me find you.

An invisible hand latched onto my right wrist, guiding me forward. I opened my eyes to make sure I didn't trip over anything and led Siobhan deeper into the crypt. I tried to see where the drop of blood from weeks ago had dried, yet it was as if it had never been there. We passed through rows of resting places, some with placards so faded by time it was impossible to even guess at how long they'd been interred.

"There's nothing here," I groaned as we reached a dark corridor that had a sloping ceiling. Siobhan had to duck a little to avoid hitting her head. We were heading underground. I could smell the dampness of earth around us.

"Maybe what you saw was just a weird dream," Siobhan offered, her golden orb bobbing over her right shoulder, casting its pale glow around us.

"No, someone was asking for my help. I'm not going to leave them to suffer."

"You heard the rumors. Some seriously bad shite happened here years ago. Maybe if someone is trapped, it's for a good reason?" Siobhan suggested.

"No one deserves to be trapped. That is cruel," I argued, taking a step forward.

Something shifted beneath my foot and the floor rippled in front of me. Out of nowhere, brilliant pinpoints of light appeared overhead, as if the ceiling had vanished, replaced by the night sky. I marveled at their beauty, my feet moving of their own accord.

"Wait!" Siobhan's voice boomed in the small space. Though I'd barely turned to see what had caught her attention when the floor completely vanished beneath me.

Panic gripped my throat, stifling the scream that wanted to escape as I turned weightless. An inky darkness loomed below me and I couldn't understand how it hadn't swallowed me whole. Something had suspended me in mid-air and when I finally found Siobhan, her pale face was blanched, her hands outstretched as she fashioned something like a lasso. She lobbed it overhand at me and by some miracle, my fingers caught the loop. She tugged it taut and began to pull me back to solid ground.

"What was that?" I gasped as the floor rippled in front of me again, returning to solid ground and the ceiling back to darkness.

"It's a leprechaun illusion," she replied, her chest heaving as she worked to slow her breathing.

"Why would that be there?"

"Much as I hate to admit it, I'd guess it's to stop

nosy students from finding out what's deeper in the crypt."

"Like a trapped soul," I murmured.

"Maybe. That spell is strong. We're lucky I could even get you out."

"What's it supposed to do?"

"Exactly what it did. Distract you with pretty faerie lights, so you don't realize you're about to plunge to your death."

"You saved my life," I said, my legs giving way beneath me.

"Well, I owed you for the whole throwing star thing."

"Is there any way to get past an illusion like that?"

"I'm not sure."

"We need to find out. I can't just keep ignoring the calls for help."

"Well, you better try, because we need to get out of here. I bet you a thousand gold coins someone is keeping tabs on that spell and will know it's been breached."

I hoped she was wrong as we retraced our steps out of the crypt. No such luck, however. Both Dr. O'Sullivan and Dr. Wren stood in front of the entrance, a brighter version of my friend's orb hovering between them.

"I had hoped I wasn't wrong to let the two of you room together," Dr. O'Sullivan sighed.

"I made her come," I said, stepping forward. "It was my idea to be out this late."

"It isn't relevant whose idea it was, you both could have been seriously injured," Wren replied in a disapproving tone.

"Take them to my office. I'll be along shortly to determine their punishment."

A lump formed in my throat as we trailed Dr. Wren along the perimeter of the pond. I prayed he wouldn't expel us for breaking into the crypt. I couldn't go back to my father having been kicked out. Especially after I'd insisted I needed to follow this path to find my own identity and honor Nai-Nai's memory.

"I would have thought you had a better head on your shoulders, Ms. Zhou," Wren said, shaking her head.

A tiny silver clock on O'Sullivan's desk ticked along, chiming the hour—1:00—by the time the Dean of Students reappeared. He sat down across from us in silence. Dark circles framed his eyes and his cheeks were drawn.

"You are both adults, so it pains me to have to tell you how foolish you acted violating the school's one out of bounds area."

"You can't blame us for being curious," Siobhan retorted.

I opened my mouth to speak, but O'Sullivan held up a hand, silencing me. "My expectations aside, I recognize that you both need to be here to learn to hone your gifts. I don't believe in expelling students who have the capacity to be educated. However, we can't have you sneaking off to forbidden areas of campus."

The door behind us opened and Wren appeared again carrying two slender bands. She started with Siobhan who looked ready to bolt as the woman slid the band around her ankle.

"This is bullshit," Siobhan protested.

"It is necessary," O'Sullivan replied. "This will deter you from returning to the crypt. You two will be monitored until you return from break in January. One would hope by that time you would have learned your lesson. Now, get out of my office."

The cool metal of the band chilled the skin of my ankle and I suppressed a shiver as I led the way back to the fifth floor. I couldn't form words to apologize to my roommate for dragging her into this mess. I'd wanted to prove myself and only succeeded in getting us both in trouble.

"Don't you dare apologize," Siobhan said once we were back in our dorm room.

"You can't be serious. I'm the reason you're under house arrest," I replied.

"I make my own decisions," she said and crawled back under the covers. "Besides, just because we aren't allowed to go exploring doesn't mean we can't still figure out who put that illusion there and how to get around it."

I admired her dedication to a cause she got no benefit from. I wasn't even sure I would find anything at the end of all this. But if she wasn't going to give up, neither would I. She was right, we had other avenues to get the information we needed.

CHAPTER NINE

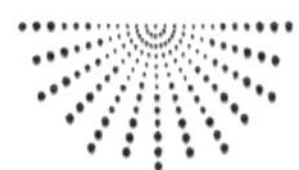

I should have been prepared for the whole school to know about our late night crypt hunt. Especially when I walked into the mess hall the next morning and Lani spotted me. Whatever conversation she'd been having died as she locked eyes on me.

"Look who was brave enough to show her face," she called and tugged on one pantleg. "Nice bling. I hear your girlfriend has a matching one."

"I heard she had to save her," one of the other djinn girls said loudly.

"Oh, yeah. Poor little wisher couldn't even recognize magic when it bit her on the nose," Lani taunted. "Some bloodline you've got."

"Just ignore her," Lee said, stepping up beside me.

"Careful who you associate with," Lani clucked.

"I pick my own friends," he answered, wrapping an arm around my shoulder and guiding me to a table.

"You didn't need to do that," I said, casually shrugging his arm off.

"She was being a bitch," he answered.

"Yeah, I'm well aware. But I'm not a damsel in need of rescuing."

"I'm sorry, I really didn't mean to imply that you were," he said.

"How does everyone know? It was the middle of the night."

"Just because people aren't supposed to be out on the grounds that late doesn't mean people aren't. Trust me, there are way more things we can do with our powers than just grant fortunes."

"So, you're telling me I was just unlucky, because we got caught."

"Exactly. But since those cuffs are supposed to stop you from getting near that place again, you don't have to worry about her getting you in trouble again."

"It wasn't Siobhan's fault. It was my idea to go there," I said defensively. "I had a dream and someone was calling to me for help. I wasn't going to ignore it. I convinced her to come along."

"Oh."

"I don't get why everyone dislikes her. I think she's cool," I added.

"She's just not what anyone expects when you think leprechaun," he replied.

"Why? Because she's strong and can handle her power?"

"Because from everything I've heard, they're always guys," Lee said bluntly.

The distinct lack of other girls that sported leprechaun abilities suddenly struck me. So, she was unusual and that drew attention. Speaking of, my roommate strode in and the room went quiet.

"Oh, admit it, you lot are all jealous I made it that far," she said loudly and got in line for breakfast.

I waited for her to join us and Lee scooted over to give her room. She eyed him for a moment before sitting down. "So, I probably should have warned you everyone would know. Miss Popular has eyes and ears all over campus."

"It's fine," I answered and looked to Lee. "We think someone living might be trapped in the crypt."

"All the stories I've heard said someone died," he countered.

"Doesn't mean there isn't someone still breathing down there, too," Siobhan argued around a bite of sausage.

"We're going to see what we can find out about who it might be and how to get past the leprechaun illusion," I finished.

"Wait a minute. Let me understand this." Lee tugged off his wire-rim glasses. "You snuck out against the rules to the one place no one is stupid enough to go even in daylight except you two. You still want to keep digging into it, even though you got caught and could have been expelled?"

I shared a look with Siobhan before we both answered, "Yes."

"Want to help us?" I asked.

"If I said yes, would you promise not to go running off halfcocked again?"

"He's got a point," Siobhan said. "We would have been better off if we'd had a plan going in the first time."

"I swear I'm not usually so impulsive," I told her. This place was testing the bounds of who I thought I was.

"Okay then, I'll help. What exactly are we looking for?" Lee posed.

"Well, like you said, someone might have died or

they thought they died there years ago and that's why it's off-limits. We need to do some research on that," I explained. "And we need to find a way past that illusion."

"I might know where to look into the illusion," Siobhan offered.

"Then you and I can do some history research," I said, eyeing Lee.

"After Wisher 101," he said. "Don't want to be late for Shen's class."

We were finally starting to learn to harness our own abilities and preparing for midterms. I still felt like I was miles behind my classmates, but I was starting to get the hang of things. At least now, the concepts didn't sound so foreign to me. We finished breakfast in silence before parting ways.

"Thanks again for agreeing to help," I said to Lee as we found our two empty seats near the back of Shen's classroom.

"You're my friend and if this stops you from getting hurt, of course I'm going to do it," he replied, patting me on the arm.

I didn't know what else to say and didn't get a chance before Dr. Shen walked in. She eyed me warily before settling in behind her desk at the front of the room. She waved her hand and a pale green aura emanated from her fingers. In response, text appeared on the board at the front of the room.

"You are going to pair off and practice summoning your unique abilities. Given that most of you are still new to your powers, that will be all that is required for your midterm exam next week. When we come back from break, we'll begin putting those skills into practice."

"I think she's mad at me," I whispered to Lee as we turned to face each other. At least it wasn't a fight to partner together. Everyone else didn't want to be caught dead working with me.

"She's just worried about you," he replied. "Do you want to go first?"

I swallowed my objection. I wasn't going to improve my skills if I didn't practice summoning my magic without seeing someone else do it first. Besides, as Dr. Shen had explained repeatedly over the last few weeks, the way our magic manifested was specific to us.

"Sure," I replied and took a deep, steadying breath.

That electrical charge I'd felt when *Nai-Nai* had transferred her powers to me had become almost a constant hum now, there below the surface. Still, it wasn't always easy to grasp and make it do what I wanted. I turned my attention inward to that thrumming energy. Oddly, it felt less active than it had even just a day ago. *Could the cuff around my ankle be suppressing access to my magic?* It seemed counterintuitive to saddle students with something that would make it harder for them to learn their craft.

Come on, you can do this.

"Remember, you must find how your magic responds to you," Shen called out from behind her desk.

'Look within,' Nai-Nai's voice echoed in my head.

I closed my eyes, trying to focus on the power within me. The cuff might be dampening it, but it couldn't eliminate it completely. I felt my fingers curl into fists in my lap as I felt the vibration of the power, she'd gifted me, rise to the surface. When I opened my eyes again, everything around me flickered and shone with a gauzy aura, like the one I'd seen on the man who'd murdered my grandmother. I turned slowly to face Dr. Shen and indeed her entire body crackled with a greenish hue. Several of the girls across the room sported silver or purple auras. It was beautiful and tears pricked the backs of my eyes. Tears of amazement. I turned back to Lee to find his brilliant orange aura flaring like a corona around his head and shoulders.

"What's wrong?" he whispered.

"Nothing. I think I just figured something out," I replied, trying to get my mind back on task. Accessing my power was one thing, getting it to work as intended was another.

I studied Lee, taking in the slope of his cheeks and the way his glasses perched effortlessly on the bridge of his nose. His gaze was dark and inviting. The longer I looked at him, the more an odd feeling welled up in my chest. I couldn't put words to it at first. It wasn't tightness or pain, but pressure. I reached blindly for a pen and paper, scribbling something down. Only once I'd laid the pen down did the pressure subside.

"Did you just do it?"

I let out a nervous hiccup of laughter. "I think I did."

I turned to study the words I'd scribbled on the page. Lee grabbed it before I had a chance, his fingers smudging the ink before I had a chance to read it. He glanced down at the dark stain on his fingers and hung his head.

"I'm sorry, I ruined your moment."

"No, it's okay. I'm sure it wasn't anything important. Probably just how you're going to do on midterms. Which is amazing, because you have all of this stuff down," I answered, taking the scrap of paper and stuffing it into the pocket of my blazer.

An awkward silence fell between us. He was busy wiping the ink off his fingers and I looked around the room again. The flaring auras were fading, but I could sense something deep within me had changed. I'd unlocked a piece of my magical puzzle now and it wasn't ever going away. For the first time since coming to Kismet Academy, I felt like I might belong.

"I should give it a try," Lee said, disrupting my thoughts.

"Right, yeah," I replied.

Even though we'd been studying basic magic all term, I hadn't had anyone else use theirs on me. The closest I'd come was the barrier in the crypt, so I wasn't sure what to expect when Lee used his ability on me.

It didn't feel like much of anything and I almost forgot he was doing anything until I watched his eyes glaze over and roll back in his head. I reached a hand toward him, afraid he would topple backward out of his chair when he blinked, adjusting his glasses as if nothing had happened.

"What did you see?" I whispered, afraid of startling him.

"I don't think it worked for me," he answered.

"You went into this weird trance. Your eyes rolled in the back of your head and everything. You're sure you didn't see anything?" I pressed.

"Nothing that makes any sense. A flash of something sparkling. I think I heard someone scream."

"What does that mean?"

"I don't know, Mae Lin. Like I told you, I don't think it worked right," he snapped.

His tone was sharp and I recoiled on instinct. Before I could say anything more, the bell dismissing class buzzed overhead. I caught sight of the note scrawled on the board reminding us that our midterm exam was the following week.

"There will be a brief written portion of the exam as well as an individual practical component," Dr. Shen announced as my classmates funneled out of the room.

If she'd made that announcement at the start of class, it would have filled me with dread. Except now that I'd had a taste of what my magic felt like in action, I clung to that feeling, committing it to sense memory as best as I could. Even in the dim hallways of the academy building, I could still see the faint auras of the people passing me by.

"Hey, I'm sorry about that," Lee called when I was halfway down the hall toward the library.

"I shouldn't have pushed you," I answered.

"I think I was just a little jealous. I mean, you managed to actually write something down. All I got were disjointed sounds and incomprehensible images."

"Maybe you just haven't quite figured out how to control it yet. Honestly, I think I just got lucky, cliché as that sounds for someone at a school where everyone grants luck."

"I think I'm just feeling a little stressed about going home," he admitted as we entered the library and found a table near the back wall beneath one of the tall windows. Late morning light filtered through, reflecting off his glasses so I could barely make out his eyes behind the lenses.

"Why would you be worried about going home? You've been doing great," I replied.

"It's not good enough, though," he replied.

"You're only in your first year, your parents can't expect you to be perfect."

"I have an older brother," he said, head bowed so our gazes no longer met.

I let that information sink in for a minute. Wishers passed their magic on when someone passed away or chose to transfer the gift for some other reason. So, my experience of getting my powers as *Nai-Nai* died wasn't that unusual.

"Did he die?" It came out in a whisper.

"No, he's still alive. My father gave me his power."

"What about your mother?"

"She doesn't have power. She's mundane."

"So, your father chose you over your brother and you're questioning his decision?"

"My brother is the favorite son. First-born, better looking. I had to practically beg my father to grant me his gift. I spent so long living in my brother's shadow. But now that I'm out of it, I worry they aren't going to think I'm doing enough with what I've been given."

"Well, you're wrong," I proclaimed and reached over to take his hand. "Take it from someone who spent the first nineteen years of their life feeling like a constant disappointment to their father, you are not a failure. You are honoring your family's legacy by being here and learning to harness your gift. Don't forget that."

His head tilted up and I caught the ghost of a smile pass over his lips. "Thanks."

"It's this place. It's changing me, making me

bolder. Old Mae Lin would have never gotten in trouble like I did," I admitted.

"You just have to promise me you'll be careful," he said and brushed a stray piece of hair out of my face. "You're too important to me and I don't want to lose you."

My heart hammered in my throat at his words. We were friends. We hardly knew one another, and here he was basically professing he had feelings for me.

"I appreciate that," I said lamely.

"But how about we get through midterms before we go racing off headfirst into danger again?"

"Deal."

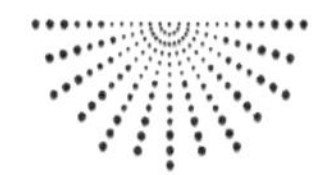

CHAPTER TEN

Midterms week was more stressful than I'd expected. Even though I was no longer rooming with Lani, she'd still found ways to make my study time miserable. She'd staked a claim to one of the largest tables in the library and had her friends there constantly, forcing Siobhan, Lee, and I to cram ourselves around a small table on the other side of the space.

"Remind me, how many classes do you have to fail before they kick you out?" Lani said an hour before our Intro to Alchemy exam.

"You were just born a bitch, weren't you?" Siobhan retorted.

"At least I know what I am," Lani spat, snapping her fingers, and vanishing in a puff of smoke.

"Don't let her get to you," Lee said, eyeing Siobhan.

"You think that drama queen bothers me?" she quipped.

Lee's jaw worked, as if he wanted to respond, but kept quiet. I knew now wasn't the right time to ask Siobhan what Lani's comment meant and she wasn't keen to share so I stayed silent.

Siobhan looked between Lee and I before she said, "Right, so I know we're focused on exams and all, but I've been doing a bit of extracurricular treks into the stacks and I think I've found something."

"What sort of something?" I breathed.

"So, there are archival records stuffed away in the back shelves about student enrollment. They say someone went missing years ago, presumed dead around the time the crypt went off limits. Fifty years or so. But there's record of another student who went looking in the crypt about twenty years back. They confirmed he died. Found a body and all."

"How does that help us?" Lee interjected.

"Because I saw some notes, looked to be from Dr. O'Sullivan saying he thinks that the student's spirit is still kicking around. If this bloke died trying to get through that barrier, maybe he's got insight into how we could get through."

"So, what, we just hold a séance and hope he's a friendly ghost?" I retorted.

"Not sure about that bit. But apparently, he left some journals behind. They're in the restricted archives."

"And you have a way into those archives, don't you?" Lee sighed.

"Might," she answered with a sly smirk. "Look, if we can sort out how to talk to this spook, then maybe we can figure out why Mae Lin is drawn there and put a stop to it."

"Even if we could figure out how to do it, we have a problem." When Siobhan arched a dark brow my direction, I stuck out my leg and tapped the cuff still encircling my ankle. "We can't get near it."

"Lucky for us they're removing them when we come back from break," she said.

"How do you know that?"

"You'd be surprised what you can overhear when instructors don't think you're listening," Siobhan replied.

"As fascinating as this is, we should get going. We don't want to be late for the exam," Lee said, already on his feet.

He was out of the library before either Siobhan

or I could gather our belongings. We fell into step side by side in the hallway leading to the exam room.

"He's just stressed out about impressing his family," I offered.

"You don't have to make excuses for him," she answered.

I opened my mouth to protest before thinking better of it. I tried to focus on running through the alchemical formulas I'd been memorizing. It was a tactic I'd used all through school and it had served me well in classes requiring formulas and equations. Though even as I sat down in my seat and pulled out a pen, my concentration waivered. My mind flitted to the thought of contacting some long-dead spirit about the possibility someone else had died on academy grounds before them. I caught Lani eyeing me and a shiver danced down my spine.

"All right, I hope you've all prepared yourselves," Dr. Wren said upon entering the classroom. She waved a hand, her fingers casting a hazy bluish hue as test papers materialized in front of each of us. "You have two hours, starting now."

I tried to block out the sounds of my classmates scribbling answers down on their test pages as I studied the first question. It asked us to explain the basic concept of alchemy.

Easy enough.

The cramming I'd been doing paid off as soon as I put pen to paper. It was like the information poured out of me. Each question seemed to build on the one before and I was able to take the pieces of the answers and link them together like a chain. Whether Dr. Wren had done so on purpose or not, I appreciated the cleverness on display.

By the time I double-checked my work on the handful of questions requiring equations and formulas, the clock at the front of the room indicated we had forty minutes left in the exam period. I could sit and go over my answers again or I could get a jump on the Wisher midterm. I needed to be in the right headspace for that one, as it was one of the only practical exams being given.

As quietly as possible, I turned in my test paper and left the room. I headed for the mess hall, intending to grab a quick snack before my next exam. The space was nearly deserted when I entered, save for a lone figure at the far side of the room.

"Ms. Zhou," Dr. O'Sullivan greeted when he spotted me. "I'm surprised to see you here. I thought you had an exam now."

I cleared my throat. "I finished early. I think I did well."

"Good. How do you find yourself settling in now that we've gotten past that business of disobeying the rules?"

Color warmed my cheeks in embarrassment. Not because I'd been caught before, but because there was the potential to get in trouble again snooping around with Lee and Siobhan.

"I think I'm finding my place," I replied. "Can I ask you something?"

He gestured for me to sit across from him and I slid into the booth. "What's on your mind?"

"The more time I spend here, the more I try to picture what it was like for my grandmother. You two were friends. I was just curious what was she like back then? Did she have a lot of friends?"

"She had a magnetic personality. A lot of people were drawn to her. I know I was." The wistful look in his eyes raised more questions than it answered. "It didn't matter to her whether you were wisher, leprechaun, or djinn, if she felt a connection with you, you were part of her small inner circle."

"That sounds like her," I replied.

"My one regret is not pushing her to be more selective. She was discerning, but no one is infallible. We can all be blinded by the mirage of magic."

He grew quiet then, lost in thoughts of the past

and I didn't want to intrude. I wasn't sure what he meant and I could sense an awkwardness rising between us. So, I broached a different subject. "Did she meet my grandfather here?"

"No. As far as I know, he was a mundane man."

I'd never known him. He'd died long before I was born. And *Nai-Nai* never spoke of him; neither did my father. Silence fell over the table, and I absently picked at a stray bit of napkin left on the table.

"What else is on your mind?" he prodded.

"It's just, I've heard rumors that something bad happened on academy grounds around the time you and my grandmother were here. I was just wondering, did she know anything about it?"

"Rumors are dangerous things," he noted. "I would focus on the present and your future, Ms. Zhou. Don't want to be late for your next exam."

He slid out of the booth, straightened his vest beneath his suit jacket and left me alone in the hall. I did my best to put the conversation out of my mind as I made my way to Shen's classroom for our Wisher exam.

MY PALMS GREW sweaty as I stepped into the hallway with my classmates, waiting to be called in for the practical portion of our Wisher exam. I spotted Lee among the crowd, but he seemed preoccupied, glancing down at a paper in his hand. I was about to make my way over and see what had him so worried when the classroom door opened and Dr. Shen stuck her head out.

"Ms. Zhou, you're up."

Lee's head whipped up at the sound of my name and for a brief moment, our eyes met. He offered me a small smile and discreet thumbs up before I followed the older woman into the room. Dr. Shen settled behind her desk which now had a second seat opposite her.

"Please, sit," she instructed.

I settled in, wiping the sweat from my palms on my pants. I took in the array of pens, chalk, and inks on the table between us along with full sheets of paper. Everyone's gift manifested differently. She had to be prepared for whatever way it expressed itself.

"When you are ready, you are going to tap into your magic and attempt to see into my future," Dr. Shen explained.

I would hate to be in her position; likely to

receive a jumbled mess of possible fortunes from novices. I hoped she wouldn't take any of them too seriously. I centered myself, closing my eyes and letting the electric current running beneath my skin to spark to life.

It crackled more intently this time, eager to please. Magic was an extension of ourselves. So, it made sense it would want to prove itself worthy of being here, because that's what *I* wanted. I felt the air around me shift, growing heavy and when I opened my eyes again, the room danced with overlapping colors clinging to every surface. It hadn't been this intense the first time I'd managed to access my magic.

Dr. Shen's aura pulsed around her body, casting a soothing green glow. At least that hadn't changed since I'd started to gain control of my abilities.

"What if I see something negative?" I blurted.

"Don't worry, I've got thick skin. Besides, I've had students warning me about my death for decades. It hasn't come true, yet."

That didn't instill me with confidence. If anything, it made me wonder what had gone wrong with those students that their predictions had been so off. Lani's taunt about failing classes rang through my mind, making me doubt myself.

"I don't mean to rush you, but I do have other students to review today," Shen noted, pulling me out of my thoughts.

I settled my gaze on Dr. Shen like I'd done with Lee a week ago. Everything around her vibrated with power and color, vying for my attention. There was so much magic to explore in this place. No, I needed to focus on the task at hand. I brushed the tip of my fingers over her knuckles and everything erupted around me.

That pressure in my chest returned, more insistent than it had been the first time. With my free hand, I reached for the nearest pen and paper, writing furiously without seeing the words. I had no concept of what I was seeing, only that I had to get it down on paper and out of my head or else I wouldn't be able to breathe.

'Help me.'

The voice from the crypt broke my concentration, like a child popping a soap bubble. My chest still ached and my hand cramped around the pen barrel. There was still more to get out, I could feel it. And yet all I could see and think about was putting a face to that voice. The pleading, hopeless nature of its call practically pulled me to my feet. The classroom vanished, replaced by the dark, cramped confines of what felt like a prison. I was stuck, locked away where no one would hear me.

The cold metal bite of the cuff around my ankle brought me back to reality and my present and the voice subsided. I blinked, the room coming back into focus. Dr. Shen watched me; her brows knitted together. *Could she sense what had just happened?*

I looked down at the paper on the desk, setting the pen aside to avoid smudging the ink as I'd done with Lee. It took ages for the words I'd written to register in my brain. *Long life is not always a gift. Beware those making promises of greatness.*

"I'm sorry, I don't know what this means," I said softly.

Dr. Shen turned the page so the text was facing up and she read it, her lips moving as she committed the text to memory. "Well, at least you weren't predicting I'd be horrifically murdered," she noted in a cheery tone.

My mouth hung open at her statement. "Someone saw that?"

She shook her head. "I'm fairly certain that student made it up so they didn't fail the exam. You may go now."

I stood; my legs weaker than when I'd sat down what felt like hours ago. The clock over the door noted it had only taken fifteen minutes. "So, did I pass?"

She looked up at me. "Grades are posted at the start of next term. But I don't see why I won't be seeing you in January."

Stepping out in the hallway felt like I'd just emerged topside after being submerged. The world tilted off its axis for a moment and I staggered sideways. A hand reached out to steady me and I turned to find Lee there. He appeared less distracted than he had when I'd gone in.

"You, okay?"

"Fine," I lied and straightened. "Good luck in there."

"I'll see you after break," he said as Dr. Shen appeared in the doorway again, beckoning the next student inside.

I left my classmates huddled in the hallway waiting for their turns. I needed to clear my head and made it as far as the front steps of the building before my body halted of its own accord. Maybe the cuff could sense my intention and enacted its strange will upon me, but I couldn't go any farther.

Yet even though I stood in the open winter air, shivering thanks to my lack of a coat, I felt boxed in, confined. The cuff might keep me away from the crypt, but the magic that called to me was stronger.

"I'm coming. I just need a little more time," I whispered to the silent air. Now I just had to find a way to summon a spirit and get through a dangerous barrier.

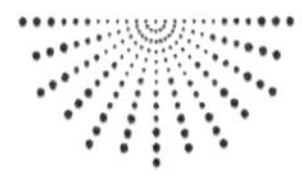

CHAPTER ELEVEN

The school grounds felt different when I returned in January. For one thing, it felt like returning home far more than going back to the city had. It had been nice to spend time with my father, but it wasn't the same without *Nai-Nai*. I could only take so much of my father lamenting that the restaurant was struggling. He hadn't come out and said it, but I could tell he'd been hoping I would come home to help run things. Or, at the very least, try my hand at writing fortunes for our customers. But I wasn't ready for that responsibility. Not yet.

"You look happy," Lee noted when he saw me in the mess hall the night before classes resumed.

"I missed this place more than I expected," I answered and slid into the booth beside him, leaving room for Siobhan to sit across from us when she arrived.

"It was pretty boring here," he said.

"You didn't go home?" I'd been so wrapped up in studying and passing midterms, the topic of our winter break hadn't really been discussed. I had assumed he would be spending it with his family.

"They decided to book a month-long vacation and I couldn't get there," he said.

My look of disbelief didn't faze him. "We have magic. You could literally portal to wherever they were," I reminded him.

"That assumes I knew where they went. They didn't bother telling me."

"That's horrible," I said, pulling him in for a sideways hug.

"It's fine. Gave me some time to dig through some of the old school archives and I found something I thought you should see." He reached into his blazer pocket and pulled out a faded color photograph. I recognized the woman in the photo immediately as *Nai-Nai*. There was a slender man with red hair that I pegged as Dr. O'Sullivan. There was a third member of their group I didn't recognize. "Does it say who that is?"

"There aren't many pictures of him. I couldn't

find a name, but there's a note on the back," he answered, flipping it over to reveal tight scrawl reading 'the trifecta, representing true peace and harmony.'

"So, whoever he is, he's djinn," I said.

"Seems like it."

"You two look cozy," Lani's voice flitted across the room, souring my mood instantly.

Just because I'd defended my friend one time against her abuse, I didn't see why she had to make me the focal point of her ire. I wasn't that interesting or important. "That's because I know how to show affection for the people I care about," I answered boldly.

"Won't your girlfriend get jealous?" Lani mocked. "Not that I'd be surprised if she doesn't show up back here."

"You really have no respect for other people," Lee said.

"Chivalrous as that is, I don't need a bloke defending my honor. I'm quite capable of doing that myself," Siobhan announced, appearing in the doorway to the mess hall. I spotted some fading bruises on her left cheek and the remnants of a black eye, too. She wore her blouse sleeves pulled down so I couldn't assess if there were any other injuries.

"What happened to you?" I hissed, gesturing to her face.

"Not here," she replied.

Lee scooted out of the booth and I followed suit, leading the way to the library. We claimed our usual study table by the back window and I took the time to study my friend in better light. The bruises weren't as faded as I'd first believed.

"Seriously, what happened?" I demanded.

"So, I may have found one of the pieces we need to have our little séance. I'd remembered some old family stories about a good luck charm that had extra mystical properties."

"And what, you got into a fight over it?" Lee prompted.

"Let's just say the person who was in possession of said charm wasn't keen to give it up and I didn't give them a choice."

I winced in sympathy. "I didn't want you to get hurt, because of all this."

"We're dealing with dangerous magics we don't fully understand. I had to haul you back from a magical barrier that would have sent you plunging to your death. I think we're beyond avoiding some scrapes and bruises."

"Where is the charm now?" Lee lowered his

voice. "Is it safe? Maybe we should keep it somewhere that people wouldn't think to look?"

"It's perfectly safe, don't you worry."

"We have another clue about who might have been presumed dead," I said, shifting the conversation back toward the photo Lee had found. He passed it over to Siobhan.

"So, you think they got into some sort of trouble, because they were all different?"

"Maybe someone didn't like the three of them being friends and did what they could to separate them?" I suggested. "Whenever the voice has called to me and I've seen pieces of whatever they're seeing, it's like I'm trapped. Confined and I can't move. I know it's not true that djinn live in bottles, but what if someone trapped this guy."

I took the photo back from Siobhan and studied the young man's features. He was handsome, with a confident smile and inquisitive dark eyes. He almost looked familiar. *Where have I seen you before?*

"So, what else do we need to commune with this other spirit?" I asked.

"I don't think anything. We just need to wait for our punishment to end then we can get back there without setting off alarm bells," Siobhan answered.

"O'Sullivan has eyes and ears all over the

grounds. He knows you two snuck out there before. What makes you think he won't notice this time?" Lee interjected. "I'm guessing if you get caught a second time, they aren't going to be so lenient."

"So, we have to be extra careful this time," I answered.

Lee opened his mouth to speak again when Dr. Wren appeared seemingly from nowhere and approached our table. "You two, please come with me," she said, gesturing to Siobhan and me.

I tucked the photo in my pocket before following the woman to Dr. O'Sullivan's office on the third floor. He sat behind the desk, dark circles still wreathing his eyes. He perked up marginally when we entered.

"I am happy to inform you both that your punishment is at an end. You've proven yourselves trustworthy and you both did exceedingly well on your midterm exams. I think we can remove those cuffs now. Start fresh for a new year."

Neither of us argued as Dr. Wren knelt down and pressed her thumb to the metal. Some unseen catch released and the cuff fell to the floor with a clatter. The instant the metal broke contact with my skin, I felt lighter. And the pull I'd sensed the first time I'd set foot on the grounds had returned.

It wasn't nearly as insistent as before, more a gentle reminder that he was still out there, seeking my help. I'd promised to come for him. I hadn't been wholly convinced it was a 'he' until I'd seen the photo of *Nai-Nai* and O'Sullivan with the third man. What had O'Sullivan told me during exams last month, that he regretted how Nai-Nai seemed to be too trusting? Had this djinn tried to harm her and she'd had no choice but to defend herself? It would be so simple to ask O'Sullivan for answers, but he appeared guarded, like talking about the past was painful. I needed answers if I had any hope of finding a way to track down the man who'd murdered my grandmother. However, I still couldn't bring myself to force this man, my grandmother's friend to relive the past. I couldn't be that cruel.

So, we would find another way; one he wouldn't approve of, but one that had to be followed. I led the way back to our dorm and Siobhan closed the door. She pulled off her blazer and rolled up her sleeves, revealing more marks on her pale skin.

"Who did that to you, Siobhan? Please, just tell me," I whispered.

"I told you, I got into a bit of a scuffle to get the charm."

"Will you at least tell me who you took it from?"

"My uncle," she replied with a shrug.

"Does the rest of your family know what he did to you?" Shock and disgust modulated my voice up an octave.

She reached over and put a hand on my shoulder with an expression that suggested she was explaining a difficult concept to a child. "Not all of us come from families where people give a shit about you."

"You don't think I can handle whatever it is?" I pointed to the closed door to the dorm. "I know people treat you like crap here. What I don't get, is why. We've been friends for months. It's time I know the truth."

"You've heard it, all leprechauns are male. Well, they take that very seriously. Point of pride that their sons have magic."

"And your family is upset they got a daughter?"

"Most days they refuse to accept that they have a daughter at all. Part of me thought I'd just skip out of coming here. The leprechaun community is tight-knit. Every bloke here knew me before I ever set foot on campus. You've been lucky not to have heard most of the names they call me. I suppose they prefer to do that in private."

"What names?"

"Just thinking them makes me sick. They hate me, because I had the misfortune to be born in the body of a girl."

Her words bowled me over. How had I not realized with all of the little jabs from Lani, and even Lee over the last few months. I could say Lee had been more diplomatic about it. Though he had still made it sound like I shouldn't be around her, because of who she is.

I wrapped my roommate in a tight embrace. "I know you don't need my validation, but you are perfect just the way you are and you are who you are supposed to be."

"Thanks," she said, patting my back.

"So, are the bruises really about the charm or just your uncle being bigoted?"

"Oh, the charm. He's actually the one person who doesn't hate me for being me. But he knows this charm is powerful and wanted me to prove I was worthy of taking it. It's kind of been the family's symbol for generations."

"We should use it as soon as possible. The less time I have to feel the pull of that place, the better."

"I don't agree with Lee on a lot of things, but he's right. We can't just go off without a plan this time. And even though O'Sullivan says he trusts us, he is going to be keeping a closer eye on us than he was before. We're off leash now, but he wants to see if we've learned our lesson."

"So, what do we do now?"

"We lay low just for a bit. Get back into the swing of classes."

The thought of waiting didn't thrill me, but she was right. We'd seen what happened when I rushed off without a firm plan in place. We couldn't afford to make the same mistake twice.

CHAPTER TWELVE

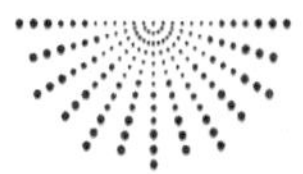

I made it two weeks before I felt the stronger pull of what I was coming to believe was a trapped djinn in the crypt. Maybe he could sense my need to find my rhythm again in this place. Though now that I had settled into my schedule, I could feel his presence, following me everywhere I went.

"This needs to happen and soon," I told Siobhan as we took our seats in Hennessey's new Introduction to Defensive Magics class.

"I think there's probably been enough time," she agreed. "But we can't do it alone. You're the one who needs to talk to this spirit if we can raise him. And you're going to need me to work the charm."

"We need Lee," I replied in a hushed tone as Hennessey walked in.

I spotted thin tendrils of lavender aura trailing behind him like coat tails. He didn't seem to notice them as he stepped up to the front of the room and waved his hands. The few people still in conversation quieted down, but he hadn't been signaling for silence. I saw bits of colored magic leap off his fingertips and stick to the floors, walls, and ceiling.

"I think we are ready for a little practical exercise today. Good to get the blood flowing," Hennessey announced. "Don't worry, no one is going to get injured. I've placed protective wards on the room. I want you to pair off and practice the defensive conjuring we've been studying."

Mercifully, no one tried to break up Siobhan and I as we moved to a corner of the room. While other students grumbled about having to actually do magic, I grinned wide at my friend. Practicing this conjuring was perfect timing for traipsing down to the crypt to summon a spirit. We needed to know how to defend ourselves and the more we did it now, the better chance we had of using it if the need arose.

"So, I guess just try to come at me?" I told my friend. Her bruises had faded to a pale yellow now and the black eye fully resolved, but I still couldn't bring myself to attack her.

"Brace yourself then," she said and took a step away. I tracked the movement of her torso and her arms as she shifted. Her weight rocked back onto her heels. I was too focused on trying to decide where her body was going to move next. I didn't see that she'd already palmed a throwing star and lobbed it at my left shoulder. It whizzed by me with a metallic whistle and I spun, expecting to find it lodged in the board at the front of the room. Instead, the point touched the wall, turned a vibrant shade of purple, melted on the spot into a dripping pool of liquid gold.

"Oy, that took me ages to get balanced just right," Siobhan protested, pushing past me, and kneeling beside the ruined weapon.

"Next time, don't bring such delicate things to class," Hennessey answered before waving his hand. The gold solidified back into its original shape. "Put it away."

She retreated to our corner of the classroom, a sullen expression on her face, but she set it on the desk just out of reach. I took a breath and waited, trying not to anticipate her movements as much this time. Instead, I focused on what her magic was doing. I could see it fiery orange around her, like an extension of her personality. It gathered around her hands like boxing gloves and when she swung her hand back, I could feel the wave of magic before she released it.

My hands moved of their own accord and I could swear I felt another pair of hands guiding me. My hand moved in the conjuring gesture we'd been studying and a shimmery golden wall sprung into being between us, halting her magic in its tracks. She blinked at me and stepped back, lowering her hand.

"Excellent, Ms. Zhou," Hennessey praised. "I see you've been practicing."

I didn't respond. It hadn't felt like I had been in control of the magic there. Part of me wanted to believe it was *Nai-Nai* somehow working through me, but it hadn't felt like her presence. Could the djinn be reaching out through this strange bond we shared?

My attempt to get Siobhan to use the defensive conjuring against me proved less fruitful. Not because she couldn't do it, but because I couldn't bring myself to harm my friend. For a fleeting moment I wondered if Siobhan had so easily thrown the throwing star at me, because she didn't trust me.

"Good effort today, everyone," Hennessey said as the wards around the room faded. "Readings are assigned. Until next class."

"I thought you were going to take my eye out with that thing," I told Siobhan as we headed back toward the dorm.

"Honestly, I wasn't even thinking. It's sort of rote. Probably shouldn't keep them on me during lessons, but, well, habits are hard to break."

"I've never seen gold just melt like that."

"That's the thing about leprechaun gold; it's strong as hell in the hands of a leprechaun. The minute someone else lays hands on it or subjects it to magic, it changes. That's how fool's gold came to be."

"See, I never would have known that if you hadn't come here," I said and nudged her shoulder.

"Guess you did get pretty lucky," she joked.

"I'll see you in a bit. I think I'm going to spend a little time in the library. Hopefully, it will be quiet and I can do some studying," I told her before retracing my steps down a few floors and then slipped into the library.

Given it was mid-morning, most people were either still in class or grabbing a late breakfast in the mess hall. I curled up in the chair at the far back corner and pulled out my phone, running my thumb along the lock screen picture of *Nai-Nai* and I at high school graduation two years ago.

The phone buzzed with an incoming call and I nearly dropped it. I'd barely used it since being here. O'Sullivan had mentioned something in passing at the start of term in September about spotty cell phone reception and I had assumed it was true.

"*bàbā*, is everything okay?" I answered after the second vibration.

"I wasn't sure I was going to get you. I thought you might be in class," he said, surprise clear in his tone.

"I'm on a break. What's wrong?"

"Nothing is wrong. Well, not really. I was cleaning out the boxes in the office and I came across some of your grandmother's journals."

"I didn't know she kept any," I replied.

"Most of it is too faded to read, but there's one part that is perfectly clear. I sent it to you. I think it might be important."

"Thanks," I said, my tone mirroring the surprise he'd expressed moments ago.

My phone beeped with an incoming image and I tapped it to enlarge. It wasn't her usual neat script. This was scrawling, messy, like she'd written it in a hurry. My father needed to rethink his definition of clear.

"Thank you, *bàbā*."

I spent the next twenty minutes trying to decipher my grandmother's scrawl on my phone screen. I couldn't make out much, except for a few words at the end of the page.

He is too powerful. I fear that one day, he will pose an unchecked danger. As much as it hurts, we must keep him contained. For his sake, and ours.

"There you are." Lee's shadow fell over me and I jumped, dropping the phone.

"You scared me," I said, pressing a hand to my chest.

"Sorry. Siobhan said you wanted to try contacting the spirit."

"We still don't have a plan about when," I reminded him.

He flashed a toothy grin. "I've been working on that. Come on."

He reached for my hand and I bent to retrieve my phone before following him. I didn't pull away as he kept hold of my hand. He'd been a little distant the last week or so. I'd just put it down to him still feeling rejected by his family for the holidays. Except maybe he'd been distant so it wouldn't look obvious when he helped us sneak into the crypt.

We found Siobhan waiting for us in the foyer on the first floor. She started for the door, but I let go of

Lee's hand and moved to put myself in their path. "Tell me the plan first."

"O'Sullivan and Shen both have current engagements. In fact, every faculty member is currently busy," Lee said proudly.

I stared at him, trying to work out if that were true. More importantly, would we be missed if we snuck off in the middle of the day. Both Siobhan and I had a break today until after lunch time before our next class. Lee wasn't the type to skip out on lessons, so I had to believe he, too, had free time.

"And how did you figure all of that out?"

"Siobhan isn't the only one who can snoop around dusty old files. While I was here over break, there weren't too many people around. I may have snuck into O'Sullivan's office and taken a look at the faculty schedules for the semester."

For someone who'd been opposed to us pursuing this whole thing a few months ago, he was proving exceedingly useful now. Without thinking, I pulled him to me and kissed him on the lips.

"Right, you two can get all mushy and romantic later," Siobhan said. "Our window isn't going to last forever."

The faculty and our classmates might be occupied right now, but that didn't mean we could just set off across the lawn without a care. Lee put a hand on each of our shoulders and I felt power ripple over me.

"I may have done a little advanced reading for Defensive Magics," he said.

A stealth spell was just what we needed as we traversed the grounds and approached the crypt. The feeling like someone was watching me tickled the nape of my neck. I fought the urge to turn and see who was there. Deep down, I knew the someone I sensed was somewhere within the confines of the crypt.

"So, how does the charm work?" I asked when Siobhan propped the door open.

"It's difficult to explain. Easier if I just show you," she answered. To Lee she said, "Stay out here and make sure no one bothers us."

"But don't you think we should all be there?" he protested.

"We'll leave the door open. You'll be able to hear everything that's going on," I reassured him. "But Siobhan's right. We didn't have a look out last time, so we didn't know we were being watched."

His face fell. "Right. Of course."

I wanted to apologize to him, but Siobhan grabbed my arm and dragged me into the cool confines of the crypt. Before I could ask her how we'd know if we were getting the right spirit, she sprinkled a circle of gold powder on the floor and pulled out a small horseshoe made of a combination of metals.

"Ancestors, hear me," Siobhan chanted. "Grant me the good fortune to find the one I seek."

She reached her hand out and grabbed me, pulling me into the circle with her and pressed the charm into my hand. "You need to think about what you want to have happen," she said.

Having no clue who the spirit was we needed to find, I did my best to comply. Slowly, the air in the circle heated up. Steam rose from the stones beneath our feet and then, in a rush of smoke, a man appeared before us. He was translucent and I could see a piece of his skull was missing. He turned to hide that part of himself thankfully.

"Who the bloody hell are you?" he spat, eyeing us both with distrust in his eyes.

"You the bloke came looking for the missing djinn?" Siobhan countered.

"Might be, what's in it for me if I tell you?"

"What do you want?" I interjected.

"You have any idea how dreadful it's being stuck

here, unable to move on, because of this bloody curse?"

"I imagine that's been very frustrating. Maybe we can help you?" I offered.

"Just tell us what happened. Why did you go looking in the first place?" Siobhan demanded.

His nose wrinkled at her, but he sighed. "Rumors say there's more than just a lost soul in here. Disappeared along with some serious power. I thought that sounded not half bad. Didn't count on the damn traps."

"You're a leprechaun, that glamour shouldn't have done anything to you," Siobhan countered.

"Wasn't leprechaun magic, girl. Now, I think I've answered enough of your questions. You want more, you're going to have to strike a bargain."

"Not likely," she replied.

"Maybe if you were more specific about what you wanted, we could do something?" I tried to assuage the spirit.

"I want out of here. You free me from this hell and you can know all the things you want," he said.

"Okay. How hard can that be?" I eyed Siobhan.

"Releasing spirits isn't in our wheelhouse. Besides, you can't just strike a bargain with him," she argued.

"But he has information we need," I reminded her.

"Maybe, but you've never granted a wish before. It always comes with a price."

"What kind of price?"

"The kind that stays with you, little wisher," the spirit said. "Free me, and you get what you want."

"How do I free you? Just say the magic word?"

"Blood, girlie," he sneered.

"No one in their right mind would make that bargain," Siobhan shouted.

"But you'd tell us everything you know about how to break this curse if we free you," I said.

"I'd tell you what I know."

Before I could make the agreement, Siobhan ripped the charm from my hand and scuffed her shoe through the gold circle on the floor. The spirit flickered out of existence.

"We were close," I said, spinning to face Siobhan.

"It's not worth risking someone getting hold of your blood," she snapped.

"He's dead. What could he possibly do?" I retorted.

"Plenty," she growled and marched out of the crypt to find Lee still standing guard. "I assume you heard all that?"

He nodded and looked at me. "It's dangerous making bargains with creatures you don't know," he told me.

"But if we don't understand where he went wrong, how are we supposed to find our way through?" I sighed.

"Look, we'll figure it out. I promise we will," Lee said, squeezing my hand.

Annoyance and disappointment crept in, souring my mood as we trekked back to the main building under the cover of Lee's invisibility magic. We parted ways, Siobhan and Lee heading for the mess hall while I trudged up five flights of stairs to my dorm room. We could have put all of this to rest in a matter of days if they'd just let me take the risk. If this spirit had really been trapped for decades and all he wanted was to be at peace, how could I say no to that?

"*Nai-Nai*, I wish you were here to guide me," I sighed as I flopped down on my bed.

What had been so dangerous about this djinn? And why would other people go looking for him? Maybe if I approached O'Sullivan again, he'd be more forthcoming.

'Don't abandon me,' the djinn's voice echoed in my head.

"I'm not. I just need more time," I breathed, knowing that he couldn't hear me.

I closed my eyes, settling back against the pillow and allowed myself to drift off. Everything melted away and I was in the crypt. I could feel multiple pairs of hands touching my body, squeezing me, and holding me down. I tried to scream, but no sound came from my mouth. An emotion washed over me so potent it made me gag on the bitterness of it—betrayal.

The scene shifted to a familiar room and a sparkling jeweled bottle sitting on a shelf. An unknown hand tapped a fingertip against the lid and it sang out in a high-pitched tone.

'Find it and free me.'

I sat bolt upright, the tone still ringing in my ears. If we couldn't get the spirit to share the information he had, then maybe we had to approach things in a different way.

CHAPTER THIRTEEN

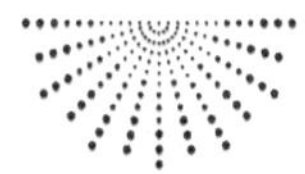

The hurt I felt at both Siobhan and Lee shutting me down lasted nearly two weeks. I was civil with them, but none of us brought up the topic of the spirit or the crypt. The djinn's voice called to me most nights now, begging me to hurry. But I was doing my best to ignore him.

"Here, look at this," Siobhan said and thrust a thick leather-bound book at me as we sat at our usual table preparing for our next Defensive Magics lesson.

I glanced at the book and immediately pushed it away. A dense article about blood curses and the uses of blood in dark magic. "You made your point already. I'm clearly not doing the bargain," I replied.

"I just want you to understand why it's so

dangerous. I don't want to see my friend risk her life when she doesn't have to," Siobhan replied.

I wanted to be angry with her for pushing this, but I appreciated that she was so concerned about my well-being. "I know you have my back. I know you both do," I said. "It's just getting worse."

Her brow knit together. "The voice? What's it saying?'

"More of the same. Begging me to help. The day we snuck into the crypt I got this sort of vision. I think it might have been a memory of when whoever was responsible trapped the djinn. All I could feel was hurt. It cut like a wound. And then I saw this bottle and it was like … I knew I needed to find it, but I'm at a loss."

"Can you describe it?"

"Sparkly. It had this strange pitch when you hit the top of it. Even when I came to, I could still hear it ringing in my ears. Every now and then I hear it again. It was somewhere that felt familiar, but I haven't been able to place it."

"Do you know what's in it that is so important?"

"Not a clue. It's not like I can have chats with the djinn. It's little snippets and phrases. Emotions and sense memories. But it's definitely getting stronger."

"Maybe we can figure out where the bottle is and why it's important."

"Why what's important?" Lee appeared, toting three covert travel cups of coffee. He was getting really good at that concealment spell.

"Mae Lin thinks we might have another angle on getting past the barrier without having to deal with the spirit problem."

"The djinn showed me a bottle. It's somewhere I know I've been before, but I can't place it."

"And it has some high-pitched tone when it's struck," Siobhan added.

"Sounds like a djinn bottle."

"I thought that was a myth that they were trapped in bottles," I noted.

"Nowadays, yeah. But there's always some truth in myth. I was doing some reading about djinn magic," he explained.

Siobhan and I shared a look and both raised brows at him. "You do know you don't have to do extra work."

"I'm curious about how other magic works. The point is you can tell a container is djinn-made by the harmonics it emits."

"Say it is a djinn bottle, do you think it's somehow linked to the one we're trying to find?"

"Probably. If you're getting visions of it, there's got to be a reason."

"We still don't know where it is," I grumbled.

"Have you tried asking the djinn for a replay?" Siobhan suggested.

"Sorry, what?"

"Well, this whole connection has felt one-sided so far. If he really wants your help getting out, maybe he should be a little clearer. Ask him what he needs from you. You've been guessing for months now."

I didn't have the first clue how to go about something like that. But it wasn't a bad idea. "Try relaxing, like you do when you are trying to detect a fortune," Lee coached.

I turned my attention inward, where my connection to the djinn and to my magic was strongest. The ripple of power beneath my skin was white hot as I tried to trace any link back to the djinn. Suddenly, in my mind's eye, I was zipping across the surface of the bond, weightless and formless, stopping at the leprechaun barrier.

"I want to help, but I need more," my voice called, echoing in the space. "I need you to show me where the bottle is."

The scene changed and my noncorporeal form sped through hallways and up sets of stairs in the academy proper. It stopped outside Dr. O'Sullivan's office. The door opened on silent hinges and there, sitting on the shelf behind his desk sat the bottle. The tone rang in my ears, getting louder until it keened.

When the library came back to me, my ears ached and my jaw throbbed from gritting my teeth. "I know where it is."

"Brilliant," Siobhan said.

I shook my head. "Not brilliant. It's in O'Sullivan's office and I'm positive he would notice if it went missing."

"So, we don't make it look like it's been pinched," she said, a mischievous glint in her eye.

"What are you suggesting?" Lee's voice was low.

"We fake it."

"You can't be serious," I hissed.

"Come on, between the three of us we can do it. It could work. We need to get a good look at the bottle, but we can manage it. A little alchemy and distracting magic. We can do it."

"What you're suggesting would take weeks. Months even to make a convincing enough forgery to trick the man who runs this entire school," Lee said.

"Well, then we better get started," Siobhan said.

My stomach did somersaults the entire time I walked to Dr. O'Sullivan's office two days later, phone stuck in my pocket. Lee had insisted the dean would be guest lecturing for the third years so I'd have complete access to the office and the bottle. I hadn't questioned why he still had access to the faculty schedules, but I assumed it was in preparation for our next inevitable trek back to the crypt.

My throat went dry as I walked up to the door, which sat ajar. It was as if Dr. O'Sullivan had been expecting my visit and made sure I had a way to get into the space without him. I paused just outside the door and held my breath, my hands shaking. I was afraid to touch the doorknob, for fear of leaving behind some evidence that I'd been there. So, I nudged the door open with my shoulder, holding my hands close to my body to avoid leaving finger-prints. It was probably a silly thing to worry about in a school full of magic, but it's where my mind went.

As the visions had showed, the bottle sat on the back shelf behind O'Sullivan's desk.

"Why didn't I notice it before?" I wondered aloud.

I tried to replay the time I'd been in his office. He'd always been sitting in his chair at the desk. The high-backed chair hid the bottle from view. He was careful where he set it, so most people wouldn't even notice it was there.

What are you doing with a djinn bottle?

I crept past the desk to stand in the small space between the back of the chair and the shelf. Despite there being little natural light in the room, the jewels and gold of the bottle gleamed in vibrant tones. Every color in the rainbow sparkled on the bottle. I snapped a few pictures of it from different angles. I didn't dare touch it. I went to stow my phone back in my blazer pocket as I retreated from the room, only to feel something fall out and flutter to the ground. I bent, scooping it up, and studying it in confusion for a moment. The ink was smeared and most of the words were illegible. It was the fortune I'd seen for Lee. In all this time, I'd forgotten I'd shoved it in there and never looked to see what it said.

The ink had been too wet when he'd picked it up and smudged all but the last word—*danger*. Not only did I now have to worry about breaking a curse on a trapped djinn, but I also had to make sure my friend didn't get hurt in the process.

CHAPTER FOURTEEN

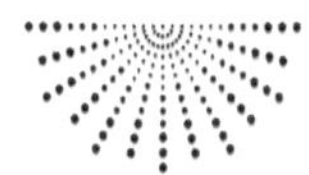

Three weeks later, we sat outside in the early spring air, contemplating the best way to forge the bottle.

"It would be easier if we had a bottle of a similar shape to work with, the gold and gems need something to adhere to," Siobhan said.

"I'm pretty sure they don't have spare djinn bottles lying around," I commented.

"Maybe not, but I'm sure the kitchens have extra serving bottles lying around. I've gone down a few times late at night and seen the staff cleaning them out and just tossing them," Lee said. "No one would miss one."

"Okay, say we get that, what do we about the gems and gold?" I said.

"Gold's easy," Siobhan said and patted her hip. "I am willing to sacrifice one of these for the cause."

"You really think you can make it look enough like the real one?"

She smirked. "That's the whole point of leprechaun gold, it's supposed to trick the eye and the senses. It will work."

"That just leaves the gems. We are going to need a dozen of them. Maybe more. All different sizes," I said, pulling up the photos on my phone again. "And that's definitely not something we're going to be able to find in the trash bins."

"Do you not read ahead in the syllabus?" Lee sighed.

"Not for everything," I retorted.

"Alchemy, we're starting to study the philosopher's stone and how to create it."

"Not that I'm arguing the stone of knowledge wouldn't be helpful in this situation, but only one person ever successfully created one," Siobhan pointed out.

"Yeah, but we'll be dealing with lots of stones. I doubt they'll miss a handful or two," Lee replied.

His theory had possibility. Wren likely had lots of stones lying around and she would need extras in case someone inevitably messed up the lesson. I looked between them. "What if we tried to grab the rejects? I have been doing a little studying on transmutation of non-metals. We could try to match the gems that way."

"Then we'd better get to work," Lee said and offered me a hand up.

We marched into the classroom in a tight trio and took spots next to each other. Rows of shiny gems in every color and shape imaginable lay on the lab benches.

"All right, before we get started, I want to temper your expectations," Wren said from the front of the room. "None of you are going to be creating the philosopher's stone today or ever."

"Then why bother doing this lesson?" Lani piped up.

"Because it is a fundamental principle of alchemy and you need to understand the basics behind it."

I pulled out my textbook and flipped to the section on the philosopher's stone. Not much was included, just the best guess as to the steps used to create it once. While it was likely at least some of my classmates would mess up their work, I wasn't willing to leave things up to chance. I had to ruin a few stones to be sure we had enough to work with.

So, I set out following the first part of the

instructions, submerging the stones in the cleansing bath, turning the burner to medium heat even though the instructions said low.

"What are you doing?" Siobhan hissed out of the corner of her mouth.

"Making sure we get what we need," I answered.

As I watched the solution bubble, the stones began to shake, like pop rocks in soda. I reached to lower the flame and suddenly, I was no longer in the classroom. I was somewhere dark, cramped, and painfully absent of other life. The sheer weight of the loneliness brought me to my knees and my chest ached as I fought to breathe.

"Please, let me go," I rasped, clutching my throat as my airway burned. It was my voice, but not. Tinges of his tone came through, too.

Please stop the pain.

The classroom came back to me just as the solution in front of me bubbled over and the stones shot up into the air, colliding with one another and combusting with a concussive 'pop.' I held up my hands to shield my face, but nothing fell. I looked up to find Dr. Wren's magic swirling around me, warding off the ruined stones.

"You need to pay more attention, Ms. Zhou," she chided and set more stones in front of me.

"She seriously could have killed us," Lani protested loudly.

"The wards in the room wouldn't have let that happen," Lee shot back in my defense.

"You don't know that," Lani sniffed and turned back to her own experiment.

"Please tell me you didn't mean to do that," he said in a whisper in my ear.

"Not exactly. I was trying to ruin them so we had some to work with, but then I was ... somewhere else and I couldn't breathe. By the time I was back here, everything had gone sideways."

"Let's just see what we can get at the end of class," he suggested.

I tried my best to focus on the assignment for the rest of the lesson instead of the fact I could have seriously injured myself and my friends. It was a monumental task it turned out I wasn't up to. Every time I reached for the burner, the sound of the stones exploding echoed in my ears and my heart hammered in my throat.

By the end of class, I'd failed to complete the assignment and I was still jumpy. I let Siobhan and Lee go on ahead. I felt I owed Dr. Wren an apology and maybe I could still muster the wherewithal to take the handful of discarded stones she'd collected.

"I wanted to apologize," I said and approached the front of the room. "I'm not usually that absent-minded."

"Absent-mindedness tends to come with a cause," she said and tossed another stone into the discard bin.

"I think I thought I knew more than I did and I overcompensated," I said. "Again, I'm really sorry I put people in danger. I never meant to."

"That's why we have wards on the classroom, Ms. Zhou. We're educators, we expect our students to make mistakes. How else are you supposed to learn?"

I gestured to the box on the desk. "I'm happy to get rid of those for you."

She picked up the box and eyed me. "You aren't going to take no for an answer, are you?"

"It would help me feel less guilty," I said, which wasn't wholly untrue.

"Sure. Not like I've got any use for them anyway."

I tucked the box beneath my arm and left the classroom behind, heading back to the dorm where I found Siobhan fiddling with one of her throwing stars. I held up the box of stones. "Well, at least one good thing came from today," I said.

"Lee said he'll get the bottle tonight. Before we

start this though, we need to know that the stones can be transmuted like you think," she said.

"I'm not sure I'm up for that right now," I replied, a weariness draping over me like a heavy blanket. "Besides, like you both keep saying, we've got time and this could take months."

"You've been the one pushing us to move on this. Why are you holding back now?"

"Because I'm scared that my friends are going to get hurt and that is the last thing I want."

"You know we can hold our own," she said, balancing the throwing star in the palm of her hand.

"You maybe, but Lee, I'm not so sure. Last term we practiced using our wisher abilities and I saw something. It got smudged before I could actually read what his fortune said, but I did get one word. Danger. Whatever is meant to happen, it's not safe for him."

"So, tell him he's out."

"I can't do that. We need him and he would never agree to it. He's just as worried about me getting hurt," I answered.

"Then we find a way to make sure we're all protected. Those defensive conjurings are a good start."

"There's something else," I said. "My father found

some old journals my grandmother kept. He sent me an image of one entry that looks like she talks about trapping the djinn."

"Wait you think your grandmother was responsible?"

"I'm not sure. She was afraid of him. And for him. It sounded like whatever they were planning, it broke her heart."

"You think O'Sullivan was in on it?"

"Probably. But there's no way he's going to admit that to us. And even if he did, what good would it do?"

"Oh, I don't know, if he was involved, he could tell us how to undo it."

"But, if he was involved, then he would have a pretty good reason to want to keep things status quo. I bet that's how he got this position. One of them needed to stick around and keep an eye on the crypt, make sure no one got in."

"I mean, he's kind of an arse, but I don't think he's the type of person to orchestrate someone's death. I doubt he was taking his crypt protecting duties that seriously," she noted.

"I guess not. But I still don't want to get him involved if we can help it. I'm connected to this djinn for whatever reason. My grandmother was linked to him. It's up to me to figure out what's going on."

"Okay, and if you're not ready right now, we wait."

I prayed the djinn could hold on just a little longer.

CHAPTER FIFTEEN

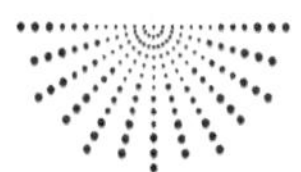

Concentration was at an all-time low by the time final exams rolled around. We'd had the djinn dust for months and had done nothing with it. I'd let Siobhan convince me that it was too dangerous. That Nai-Nai's journal entry and the fortune I'd read for Lee were harbingers of dangerous things to come. The fact this scared my friend with a penchant for talking with her weapons, I'd given it some credence.

Except the sound of the djinn's increasingly distressed calls echoing in my head day and night were driving me mad. Siobhan had been curing our fake bottle for the last week and it was almost ready to make the switch.

"One of you has to do it. I can't," I said, barely able to lift my head from the table in the mess hall the day of our last set of exams—defensive magics and alchemy.

"She hasn't been sleeping," Siobhan noted to Lee.

"How can I? He won't shut up in my head," I groaned.

"I'll do it," Lee offered before passing me a thermos. "Drink this. It should at least pep you up enough to get through exams."

I downed the tangy tea in the thermos and immediately sat up, as if someone had hooked me up to a charger. Everything around me took on a distinct vibration and auras flared.

"What was in that tea?" I said, running my fingers along his arm.

"Just a recipe my mom used to give me for long nights studying," he answered.

"Well, as soon as we've finished exams and you've nabbed the bottle, we meet at the crypt and get this over with," Siobhan said.

"Agreed." I darted from the booth, bouncing on the balls of my feet. Time to tackle these exams.

Alchemy was up first and I paced outside the classroom, waiting impatiently for Dr. Wren to let us in. I spotted Lani out of the corner of my eye, but couldn't be bothered to let her obvious irritation dampen my mood. We were finally going to get answers and the djinn could stop taking up every available moment of my focus and energy.

"Come in," Dr. Wren called, opening the door.

I was first into the classroom, looking around at the stations set up. I sat at one nearest the door and watched my classmates enter, taking up seats at other available stations. Where the midterm had been all theoretical, I was eager to show what I could do in the practical skills assessment.

"You will have one hour to turn the base metals in front of you into gold."

We'd been studying the process of transmutation all year and I'd been soaking it up like a sponge. Having to manipulate leprechaun gold to resemble the metal of the djinn bottle hadn't been bad practice, either. I bounced on the balls of my feet as I waited for the clock to start.

"Begin."

I studied the three objects in front of me—a chunk of silver, an iron sphere, and a call coil. An hour wasn't long enough to completely reform all three into the purest form of gold possible. In fact, in all of my studying, I'd never seen iron transmuted successfully. Maybe that was part of the test; to know what we could and couldn't change.

I lit the flame on my burner then set the silver and the copper to heating. I glanced across the room at Siobhan. Her hands were firmly shoved in her pockets as she waited for her metals to liquify. She clearly didn't want a repeat of the lesson that had ended in us becoming roommates. As I waited for my metals to follow suit, I rolled the iron ball in my fingers. It trailed an electric current over my skin.

'*A catalyst,*' the djinn's voice echoed in my head.

If he was going to constantly be in my head, having him give me pointers on exams wasn't the worst thing. I reached beneath the lab bench and found a small hammer, splitting the sphere in half. It shimmered with gauzy white light from its center as I dropped one half into the copper mixture, watching the light dance across the surface like mist. The copper stilled for a moment before leaping up toward my hand, leeching magic from my fingertips before settling back down in the pan, no longer orange, but pristine yellow gold.

I pocketed the other half of the iron sphere and did my best to transmute the silver as we'd been instructed. I had to hope Wren wouldn't penalize me for not having three gold objects in the end.

By the time the hour was up, I'd cooled both my copper-iron combo and the silver. The second was passable as gold. I could see the impurities within it as Wren came around and collected our products, labeling each carefully.

"That was horrible," Siobhan said and I noticed she looked paler than normal.

"It wasn't so bad," I told her. "I mean, I'm sure she had to know that we couldn't actually change the iron."

"I can't believe she used that stuff," Siobhan railed. "She has to know leprechauns are allergic." She showed off her hands and I saw tiny angry red marks on the pads of her fingers.

"Didn't you wear gloves?"

"I'd need something thicker than what she gave us to have any chance of not ending up breaking out in hives," she grumbled.

I looked around for Lee as we made our way to Hennessey's class for our last exam. I hadn't seen him leave Wren's exam, but he'd gotten good at hiding himself. For all I knew, he'd walked right past me and I hadn't noticed.

"Where is ..." I stopped mid-question as Lee appeared, his bag pressed oddly to his chest.

He nodded toward an empty alcove up the hall-way. Once we were blocking any onlookers from snooping, he showed us the bottle. It looked remark-ably like the one we'd put together. But, when I reached out and pressed a finger to it, I could feel the reverberations of the tone in my eardrums.

The tea and the anticipation of putting this to rest buoyed me as I walked into Defensive Magic. The room had been cleared of furniture. I could see and feel the protective wards already in place.

"Your exam is simple. You will each be faced with an assailant. You will have three tries to disarm and defend yourself. You must succeed at least once to receive a passing score," Hennessy announced.

Before anyone could ask for clarification on how we'd be facing opponents, bright blue squares of light ignited on the floor, shooting up barriers between students until we were isolated. I couldn't even hear my classmates anymore. All that remained was a shadowy figure approaching me, shifting weight from foot to foot.

"I'm not falling for this again," I said and focused on the magic and where it concentrated. I flexed my fingers, ready to cast the conjuring we'd been working on since January. It had developed from a simple blocking maneuver into a way to disperse an oncoming attack. It was almost like a dance.

The figure's magic pooled not in its hands as I expected, but in its feet. I crouched low; hands held out at the ready. When it lunged at me, its foot even with my head, I dodged to one side and deflected the magic away from my body, sending the figure off balance.

"One down," I reminded myself which meant I'd already passed the exam.

Before I had time to recover, the figure was back on its feet, this time the magic came at me from above, as if it had lobbed a volleyball. I threw my hands up too late to block it and it knocked me to the ground. The figure advanced on me and I held my hands palms out, fingers splayed as its attack coiled around its hands and its mouth. A wave of power hit me, but this time I was ready. It rebounded off my shield and whatever the spell was meant to do to me, took out the figure.

I expected to be able to leave once I'd completed my three attempts and yet the barrier remained. So, I sat there, counting the minutes until the test ended. The invigoration from the tea was waning and the persistence of the djinn had returned. He'd been quiet as I completed my exams. At least he could be considerate some of the time.

Finally, after far too long, the barriers came down. I saw several of my classmates—Lani among them—with blotchy faces. My gut told me she hadn't done nearly as well as she'd expected. Had she failed completely? I locked eyes with Siobhan and then Lee. It was time to break this curse.

CHAPTER SIXTEEN

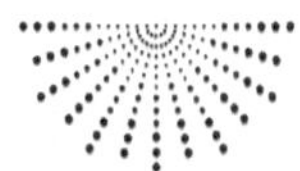

The end of exams served as our best distraction to sneak out to the crypt. Everyone was either heading back to their dorms or the mess hall for relaxation and no one would miss us. The faculty would be busy starting to grade exams. I led the charge this time, pulling the door open and stepping through without hesitation.

I looked to Siobhan and asked, "How do you beat a leprechaun illusion?"

"I'm not an expert," she retorted. "But usually it's about finding how the magic is manipulating you. What is it trying to stop you from doing? Then just do the opposite."

"So, what, we're supposed to just go the other

way, because we want to get through?" Lee suggested.

"No," Siobhan countered.

"When I first encountered it, it ended up being a giant hole in the ground that I nearly fell in. Whether I actually would have fallen through or not is anyone's guess, but it's possible if I don't think I'm going to fall, I won't," I said.

"Looks like the wisher girlie got smart."

We all turned as one to find the spirit lingering just in front of where I'd found the barrier the first time. I glanced at Siobhan. "Did you bring the charm?"

"Nope. Didn't think we'd need it."

The spirit flitted closer to us, bending down close. "You rethink my bargain?"

"She's not giving you her blood," Siobhan said, putting herself in his path.

Somehow, I doubted she could stop him if he wanted to get to me. He glared at her, but looked at me. "I'll give you this little piece for free, as a gesture of good faith. The traps in this place are leprechaun and djinn made. You'll need their magic to pass through. But you'll need something else I didn't have."

'Hurry, Mae Lin. Please hurry.'

"What else do you need? What were you missing?" I pleaded.

"That's all I'm giving you," he said.

Before either of them could stop me, I grabbed one of Siobhan's throwing stars from the case on her hip and dragged the point across the back of my forearm. "I wish for you to pass on from this plane." I flicked the blood in his direction.

As soon as it hit, he shimmered and turned bright white. "I didn't have you," he said before vanishing.

"You shouldn't have done that," Siobhan said, snatching the weapon back.

"At least we know he's gone," Lee said, pressing a cloth to my arm to staunch the bleeding.

"What did he mean, he didn't have me?"

"Let's figure that out after we know we can get through the barrier," Lee said, ushering me forward.

The barrier appeared in front of us, shimmering and inviting. I felt that same sense of longing to follow its light, but I knew I couldn't go in without a clear head. I took a step back, bumping against Siobhan. It was enough to divert my gaze upward and I saw a missing piece of ceiling that could have very easily crushed a man's skull when he tried to get through the barrier.

"So, I have to just believe I can get through?" I said, eyeing Siobhan again.

"That's the hope."

"I know what he meant," Lee said, his voice dropping a few notes as I turned to see him pressing the bloody cloth to his palm. His skin came away red as he pressed it against the barrier. "Your grandmother helped place this curse and her magic is in your blood. We need the original wisher's blood. And you just made a donation."

Before I could say anything, he disappeared through the barrier.

I stood there beside Siobhan staring at the space Lee had occupied moments ago. *What just happened?*

"What are you waiting for? We have to go after him," Siobhan said, pushing me toward the barrier.

As soon as I got close, my left arm throbbed and it almost pulled me through. I grabbed for Siobhan's hand, but my fingers missed and I couldn't get to her before the barrier swallowed me.

There was no freefall this time. Only solid ground beneath my feet. This part of the crypt was darker, colder than the rest. I could feel the decay and neglect. No one had been here in decades.

"You're going to be free," I heard Lee say.

"No. Not this way," the djinn's voice was hoarse and for the first time in nearly a year, it wasn't in my head.

I sprinted in the direction of their conversation and found Lee standing over the djinn, still locked in some sort of suspension spell. He held the djinn bottle he'd stolen from O'Sullivan's office.

"What are you doing?" I demanded.

"What I came here for," he answered.

Lee raised his free hand toward me and a swirl of grey aura shot from his fingers. They wrapped around me like a vice, squeezing so I couldn't move.

"Stop," I protested, fighting fruitlessly to free my hands. The thrum of my own magic pulsed in my chest, wanting to be free; needing to help and finding no way to fight him.

"I'm sorry it has to be like this, Mae Lin," Lee continued, stepping closer to the trapped djinn. He tipped the bottle over his cupped palm. Tiny grains of pink dust pooled there, clinging to his skin and I watched the djinn recoil from it.

"You were helping me. You were my friend," I said. Anger burned like acid in my throat and it was enough to spark my power, shattering his spell around me.

"Sometimes I forget you don't know our history. My grandfather was an exceptional wisher and student, but your grandmother always had to show him up. He vowed one day; we'd be the better, stronger family. And I swore to my father that I would be the one to bring that honor to us. And I succeeded." His words were a betrayal, yet the expression on his face was conflicted.

"By lying and manipulating people? I trusted you." I stepped up to the djinn and for the first time, I was able to take in his features. He was grimy and gaunt and I could see the preserved handprints of those who'd imprisoned him.

"I'm so sorry it took me this long to find you. And I'm sorry that my grandmother did this to you. She had no right."

"You really should have paid more attention. Or spent any time in the restricted archives, Mae Lin. This djinn was one of the most powerful of his kind in generations. He could have done amazing things. And now he's going to. For me."

"I would rather die," the djinn spat.

"Well, I have always wondered what happened to a djinn who granted all of their wishes."

"I'm not going to let you use another human being as a weapon," I retorted, making a grab for the bottle.

"You think I want to hurt people?" Lee scoffed. "People will be thanking me for curing cancer and ending world hunger. With his magic, I can cure every ill that ails the world. You can't argue with that."

"It's still wrong."

'Free me. Before he can.'

"I'm sorry. But you're not going to stop me." He lifted the handful of dust to his mouth and blew it at the suspension spell.

The djinn fell to his knees and I reached out a hand to steady him, but somehow my body moved in slow motion. Every muscle felt like I'd run it ragged and had reached its breaking point. Lee looked at his wrist, as if checking the time. "Right on schedule."

"The tea," I said.

"For what it's worth, I can wish for you to forget all of this. You could go back to your mundane life, not remembering any of this."

"Don't you dare," I ground out, forcing myself to stand.

I'd been afraid to use offensive magic on my

friends, but in this moment, Lee was no friend. The anger and betrayal that had been such a crushing weight for the djinn sitting before me coursed through my body now, building up my magical reserves until everything shone in vibrant color. I felt something warm in my pocket and dipped my fingers in to find the iron sphere half. It was relatively harmless to wishers, but it could make for a good distraction.

"Then I guess I'll have to make sure you can't interfere with my plans," Lee said, holding up one hand.

I didn't give him the chance to make the first move. I threw my hands up in the defensive conjuring, ready to disperse any spell he sent at me. I lobbed the chunk of metal at him, forcing it to change its state of matter as it passed through my shield. It exploded in his face, momentarily blinding Lee and he dropped the djinn bottle.

"I can help you," the djinn called.

"Then do it," I said as Lee started peppering my defensive shields with a volley of blows. The shield dispersed them, but my arms shook with the effort to maintain the magic.

"You need to wish me free."

"I'm pretty sure that's the last thing I'm supposed to do," I said as my right knee buckled and I faltered.

My magic sputtered around my right side as pain radiated up my back and not my chest. I realized too late he'd started throwing magic around the edges of my shield. He'd had more time to learn his craft. He'd been preparing for this moment for years.

My magic waivered and in that moment, I could see his next attack coming. I was powerless to stop it. A shockwave of energy hit me, sending me slamming into the nearest wall. Air fled my lungs, black spots danced in my vision, and a groan escaped my lips.

'Get up and fight,' the djinn demanded in my head.

It wasn't right that I couldn't beat Lee in a fair fight. But if wishing the djinn free meant that Lee couldn't use him as a weapon, then whatever consequences came with it were worth it.

"What's your name?" I rasped, making eye contact.

"Bashir."

"Bashir, I wish you free."

Brilliant silver light erupted from the center of Bashir's body and the gaunt look vanished, replaced by strong muscles. He cupped his hands together, a sphere of swirling energy materializing instantly. Lee seemed unaware as he advanced on me. He grabbed me by the front of my shirt, hauling me to my feet.

"I really wish you hadn't done that." I noted the faintest tremor in his hands as he looked at me; like he was afraid to use his magic again. "If you kill me, Siobhan is going to hunt you down," I said, blood dribbling out the side of my mouth.

"What the *hell* is going on?" Siobhan demanded.

Lee had enough time to turn toward her before Bashir's magic collided with him, sending him slamming into a wall, too. Lee crumpled to the ground as Siobhan raced to my side.

"Lee lied to me. The whole time he was using me to get in here, to get to the djinn to use his powers," I said, my body aching.

"I should have known something was off. We need to get out of here."

"We are bound, Mae Lin," Bashir interrupted.

"No, I freed you. You specifically told me to do that."

"All wishes come with a cost. You need rest and recovery. And no one can know what happened here today. Reset the wards. I will return."

Before I could protest Bashir vanished. I turned

toward Lee's body to find that he was already on his feet again, scrambling for the djinn bottle.

"Oh, hell no," Siobhan said and flicked a throwing star so it landed half an inch from his outstretched hand. "Next one won't miss."

He yanked the star out of the ground and lobbed it back at her. It stopped midair. "Nice try."

Unfortunately, it was all the time he needed to snatch the djinn bottle, pour out a handful of dust and sprinkle it over himself, vanishing from sight.

CHAPTER SEVENTEEN

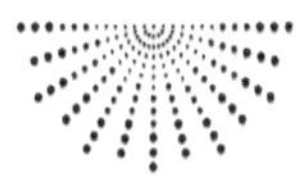

I awoke two days later in the infirmary to find Siobhan sitting next to my bed in a chair. My whole body still ached from the fight with Lee. I still couldn't wrap my head around the fact he'd betrayed us.

"How are you feeling?" Siobhan propped her chin in one hand.

"Confused," I answered, my throat dry. "I still can't believe he did that."

"He fooled us both, Mae Lin," she said and moved to sit on the end of my bed. "It could have been so much worse if you hadn't gotten to the djinn first. I can't imagine what Lee would have done if he'd had mastery over him."

The odd connection I'd felt to the djinn, Bashir,

had only intensified when I'd wished him free. I couldn't put words to the feeling, but I knew he wasn't truly free. Sure, he was no longer a prisoner to the crypt, but there was still some strange connection between us.

"No one's seen the coward in days," Siobhan continued.

"Have you reached out to his family?"

"O'Sullivan got quiet when he realized I was listening. I think he figures it's a police matter for now. Treating it like a runaway kid."

"He was trying to bring honor to his family. As much as it broke my heart to see him turn on me, I understand why he'd do it."

"He wasn't really your friend, Mae Lin. He doesn't deserve your sympathy."

But maybe he deserved some empathy.

"Does O'Sullivan know what happened?"

Siobhan leaned in close and whispered, "I managed to put things to rights, so it all looks like nothing was disturbed. As far as anyone knows, he went looking to break the curse and failed, because we stopped him. No one should know what happened."

Heavy footsteps halted our conversation as O'Sullivan appeared around the edge of the half-drawn curtain. I sat up as best I could with the ache in my ribs and chest. He waved a hand. "Please, no need to get up on my account."

"Any word on where Lee is?"

"I'm afraid not. But I wanted to check on you and see how you were feeling. And to assure you that these types of things are a rare occurrence on campus."

"All that matters is he didn't succeed," Siobhan offered.

"We know there was someone trapped down there that Lee was after. A djinn. The one you and my grandmother were friends with," I said. Even if we were trying to keep the secret of Bashir's release from confinement, it didn't mean I couldn't get O'Sullivan to admit his complicity in trapping him in the first place.

"Losing friends is never an easy thing, especially when they are such dear friends," he said, unshed tears sparkling in his eyes. "I'll let you two rest. I hope you'll be feeling well enough to join everyone for the end of term celebration."

In all the excitement, I'd completely forgotten the end-of-term festivities, not to mention final grades. Magic had changed my life in so many ways, but even that could change my desire to excel at this endeavor; to prove to my father that this was the right choice.

"Any idea where our djinn friend went?" Siobhan asked a few minutes later.

"I have no idea," I replied, sinking back against the pillows. "For all I know, he's off enjoying fresh air for the first time in decades. Wake me up when it's time for the celebration."

BY THE TIME the celebration rolled around a few hours later, my body had recovered sufficiently that I could get out of bed without feeling ready to keel over after a couple steps. Siobhan dragged me down to the auditorium where exam scores were posted in long rows. I spotted Lani a few people down. She let out a disbelieving wail and stormed off.

"Karma would be so sweet if that shrew was no longer in our lives," Siobhan said as she ran her finger down the list of names until she found her own. She trailed it across to the list of courses she'd taken. "Well, not the best scores, but good enough to pass."

We moved down the wall and found my name. I let out a sigh of relief at the scores. I'd earned mostly

Bs and an A in Intro to Alchemy. Given everything else I'd dealt with this year, I would take it as a win.

"Guess we'll both be back next year," Siobhan said with a smile.

"If they let second years pick roommates, I know who I want," I said and wrapped an arm around her shoulders as we followed the crowd out onto the grounds. We fell in line with the rest of our year as an enormous spread of food appeared laid out on long picnic tables. Most of the older students were out of their uniforms and back in casual clothes as they lounged, chatting together in clusters.

Siobhan and I took our food over toward the nearest edge of the pond, sitting side by side and faced the crypt across the water. It had called to me for so long, I still expected to hear his voice begging me for help. I had come here looking for answers to who had killed *Nai-Nai* and while I hadn't gotten any closer, I had managed to uncover the truth of her past. My gut told me the two were connected. At least it was a start.

"It feels strange to speak this way," Bashir said, his voice clear and right beside me.

I dumped my plate onto the grass beside me as I turned to see him standing there. No one else seemed to notice his sudden appearance. "No one knows you're free. I think it's safer if we keep it that way. So, maybe don't go popping up at random?"

"I told you I would be back," he noted.

"What I don't understand is why. You were friends with my grandmother. Are you just linked to the magic in me?"

"I don't know. But we need to find out and quickly. There is darkness brewing and if we cannot break this bond, I fear we will all be doomed."

QUICK AUTHOR'S NOTE

CREATING the world of Kismet Academy was quite the experience. It delved into cultures and characters that were outside of my wheelhouse. But I enjoyed getting the chance to discover who these characters are. I can already tell you I'm getting strong spin-off vibes for Siobhan.

WHEN I FIRST STARTED WORKING ON this series, I hadn't quite realized that she would have a murder to solve. One where she knows how it happened but still can't put a name to a face. But, I came to realize that many of my stories center around mystery of some sort and it gives her a stronger drive to learn to harness her powers. I promise, she will get her chance to uncover who kicked off these heartbreaking series of events. Second year at Kismet Academy is going to be a wild ride.

Turn the page to get a sneak peek at *Luck Breaker*.

Luck Breaker

Wish in one hand, djinn in the other…

Secrets, lies, and visions of a coming darkness haunt Mae Lin as she reenters Kismet Academy for her second term. But her connection to Bashir has grown increasingly stronger, and with it, her wisher magic...and her feelings for the djinn. She's just not sure if she can trust them to be true.

But what she does trust are the recurring visions she and Bashir share. The darkness she foresaw resurrects an enemy from Bashir's past and a rivalry he thought long extinguished. One that threatens all their lives and the academy itself.

With nothing more to go on, Mae Lin must reunite with old friends and an enemy and use their collective magic to find a way to stop the oncoming storm. But the fortune her grandmother made looms over her still, and if it comes to pass, Mae Lin will be in even greater danger. The kind she may not be able to overcome.

Luck Breaker *is available on all storefronts - find it on your favorite store today!*

OR

Buy direct from me and get the complete series box set! Bundle and save 20% with code **BUNDLE20** here.

ABOUT THE AUTHOR

Sarah Biglow is a *USA Today* bestselling author. She lives in Massachusetts with her husband and son. She is a licensed attorney and spends her days combatting employment discrimination as an Investigator with the Massachusetts Commission Against Discrimination.

You can find an up-to-date list of all my books here

www.ingramcontent.com/pod-product-compliance
Lightning Source LLC
Chambersburg PA
CBHW031015190726
48286CB00003BA/858